STUCK WITH S'MORE DEATH

A JILL ANDREWS COZY MYSTERY

NICOLE ELLIS

1

_____

"I don't know, Jill. I still think it would have been fun to go camping somewhere in the mountains," Adam said as he rummaged in his dresser drawer for a pair of shorts.

I stopped folding a pile of kids clothes to take with us on our vacation and stared at him. "We have a nine-month-old. Tent camping sounds miserable."

He shrugged. "I'm sure we could have made it work."

I rolled my eyes and packed the neat piles into the suitcase that lay open on our bed. In as calm a voice as I could muster, I said, "I'm sure we could have, but I think we'll have more fun staying in the cabins at the Thunder Lake Resort. Besides, I'm looking forward to seeing Leah again."

He looked up at me. "You haven't seen her since you worked together, right?"

"Yeah, she left about a year before I had Mikey. When she and her husband quit the rat race to buy a campground in Eastern Washington, I thought she was crazy."

He raised an eyebrow. "That's a big change."

"I know." Owning a campground was vastly different

than working as a marketing executive at a firm in down-town Seattle, but her husband, Del, was an avid outdoorsman and had talked her into it. "But she seems to be thriving out there and making the resort a success. Desi and I had to make these reservations a year ago."

"Hmm. Well, maybe next year we can go tent camping?" He regarded me hopefully.

"Maybe." I didn't want to tell him that there was very little chance that I'd voluntarily go somewhere that didn't have running water and flushing toilets. Then again, there were some nice campgrounds nowadays. Perhaps there was room to compromise. Besides, next year was a long way off.

A pang of realization hit me. Our kids were growing so fast that, in truth, I didn't know what would be fun to do with them next year. Ella would be walking soon, and Mikey would probably kill to go to Disneyland. I forced myself to take a deep breath. They weren't exactly leaving the nest anytime soon, and we'd have many fun family vacations in the years to come.

"We're at least going to get to go hiking, right? Now that I'm home more, I'd really like to get back to hiking more often. Why bother living in such a beautiful area if we're not going to enjoy the outdoors? We went often when I was a kid, and I'd like for Mikey to start experiencing the great outdoors too."

I held up a pair of pint-sized hiking boots. "I bought these for Mikey so you can go with him."

His face lit up. "Thanks, honey." He grabbed his stacks of clothes off the bed and placed them in the other suitcase. "I'll pack my shaving kit tomorrow morning. Is there anything else you need me to do tonight? I had a new client come in today, and I want to make sure I have as much done on their case as I can before we leave." He looked like a little kid waiting to be excused to go play.

I smiled at him. It was nice to see him excited about work again. He'd recently left the law firm he'd been with for years and started his own practice in downtown Ericksville. He hadn't been inundated with clients yet, but the change in his attitude about work had been amazing.

"Nope, I've got it from here. I'm going to check on the kids and then log into work for an hour or so myself."

"Great." He scurried out of the room.

I zipped up the two suitcases and stacked them in the corner of our room. Leah had told me that they provided linens and kitchen equipment for the small cabins, but I didn't know what else we'd need. Maybe plastic inner tubes for playing in the lake? I jotted it down on my notepad. We were planning to leave around noon the next day, so I'd hunt for the sand and water toys in the garage after breakfast and then throw them into the car.

When I walked past his room, Mikey was sleeping soundly with his face illuminated by a Mickey Mouse nightlight. I continued on to Ella's room to check on her in her crib and put my hand on her chest. She smiled at me in her sleep, melting my heart.

It had been a long summer, and as much as I'd been enjoying my new job at the Boathouse, the event center owned by my in-laws, I needed a break. I was looking forward to spending time with my family. My sister-in-law Desi had a four-year-old son as well and a three-month-old baby. She and her husband Tomàs could use a break, and Mikey was excited to spend a week with his cousin Anthony at the lake.

I went downstairs, sat at my desk in the living room, and fired up my laptop. My mother-in-law, Beth, and father-in-law, Lincoln, would be holding down the fort at the Boathouse while I was gone. Still, I had to respond to a few clients about their events before we left. My stomach twisted a little. I'd become so involved in my work that it worried me to leave it behind for nine days. Probably a sign that I badly needed this vacation.

One of the bigger events I had on the horizon was the town's annual haunted house. In past years, it had been held in a local warehouse, but the building had recently been converted to apartments, leaving the event without a venue. We'd given the town a huge discount to have it at the Boathouse, but Beth and Lincoln figured it would be good for business. Also, they were active members of the community and felt it was their civic duty to help out with the big event.

I admired my in-laws' dedication to their community and I'd been excited when Beth asked me to manage the event. However, working with Angela Laveaux, the person who was organizing the haunted house, was another story. From the first time I'd called her to chat about the event, she'd been full of grandiose ideas and time-consuming demands. She'd even walked into the main room at the Boathouse during a wedding reception—interrupting the groom's toast to his new wife. She'd claimed that she'd entered the room by mistake, but she'd stayed a few minutes too long to make that appear true and I had a sneaking suspicion that she wanted to see how well we were able to execute a client's vision for their event.

I'd worked with some tough clients, but Angela might even be worse to work with than Nancy Davenport, the preschool PTA president and my archnemesis. I flipped through the notes I'd written in my notebook and confirmed that all important dates were logged on my schedule. The haunted house was scheduled to run for the entire week leading up to Halloween and would be highly visible in Ericksville. Everything looked in order, but I felt bad leaving Beth at Angela's mercy while I was gone. Then again, Beth had been running things at the Boathouse long before I started there and was perfectly capable of dealing with any type of difficult client.

I shut the lid of my computer and pushed it to the back of the desk. I was going away for a week and this was the last time I planned to think about work. Adam and I had taken a couples trip together for our anniversary in June, but we'd never gone anywhere with both of the kids. School would be starting soon for Mikey and I expected Adam's commitments to his practice to increase in the near future, so our vacation to Thunder Lake Resort might be the last chance we had for a while to get away as a family. We were badly in need of some quality family time and I wasn't going to let anything get in the way of that.

_____

2

The next morning, I still felt as tightly coiled as a spring. It was funny. Vacations were supposed to be relaxing, but the preparations beforehand were incredibly stressful. I didn't remember feeling like that before having kids, but I suppose I only had myself to take care of back then. It seemed like with each kid, the stress—and gear required—had been multiplied by a factor of four.

I checked my packing list again and reassured myself that there were only a few last-minute items to add. After Goldie finished his breakfast, I'd throw his food bowls, kibble and leash into the car and I'd be done packing for him. Dogs were so much easier than kids. I'd briefly considered bringing Ella's Exersaucer, but Adam had vetoed that. I'd settled on her Pack 'n Play, bouncer, and stroller. Even with those few bulky items, the car-top carrier might be needed. I scribbled a note about it on the bottom of my list.

I washed off the kitchen counters and eyed the back of Adam's head. He and Mikey were eating buttered toast on the couch while watching cartoons. Ella sat in her bouncer close by on the floor, watching the animated characters intently. This was my chance.

"Honey," I called out. Adam didn't turn. I walked over to him and tapped him on the shoulder. I really hoped he had everything under control so I could sneak out to grab a cup of coffee in town by myself before getting into the car for a long road trip with two small children and a cranky husband.

He finally looked up. "Hey. What's up?"

"I'm going to walk down to see Desi, ok?" I leaned across the back of the couch so I was more in his line of sight.

"Sure. We're still leaving at noon, right?"

I could see him watching the show out of the corner of his eye.

"Yes." The kids' eyes were glued to the TV. I didn't like having them watch so much television, but in this case, it was buying me some much needed time to myself. "Hey, we might need the car-top carrier. Is it accessible in the garage?"

I had his full attention.

"I think so, but how *much* stuff are you bringing anyway?"

I jutted out my chin. "Babies have a lot of gear."

He shook his head. "I'll get it out of the garage." He motioned to the door. "Go have fun. Say hi to Desi for me."

"Bye, honey. Love you, kids." I grabbed my purse and hurried outside before anyone changed their mind about letting me leave. Leaning against the front door, I took in the view of Puget Sound and the town of Ericksville below our house, which sat high up on the hill. Desi owned the Beans-Talk Café, housed in a converted lighthouse keeper's cottage. Her baking skills were top-notch and my mouth watered just thinking about her baked goods. It would be so peaceful to eat a pastry and drink a cup of coffee at one of the outdoor tables overlooking the lighthouse grounds and Puget Sound. I quickened my pace. The faster I got there, the more time I'd have to relax and—maybe, if I was lucky —read the paper uninterrupted.

When I reached the café, all of the outdoor tables were occupied. I tried to convince myself that it didn't matter and I could relax inside just as well, but I knew it wouldn't be the same. There was something magical about sitting outside, feeling a gentle breeze flowing by and hearing the sounds of the boats cutting through the waves.

I didn't see Desi anywhere, but I ordered my coffee and a piece of coffee cake at the counter from Desi's assistant. After she handed them to me, I turned to see if there were any vacancies in the outdoor tables, but they were still full. I hesitated, unsure of where to sit.

"What's wrong?" Desi asked as she approached me.

"Oh, nothing." I stared down at my coffee cup. Even the cute heart the barista had swirled in the top of my latte wasn't lifting my spirits.

She put her hands on her hips. "Jill. You look way too glum for someone holding a cup of java and a piece of my coffee cake."

"It's silly, but I had this picture in my head of eating outside today. I need to decompress a little after making it through my packing lists."

She laughed. "I felt the same way this morning. How is it possible that such small children could need so much stuff for a week away? Anyway, I left the kids with Mom this morning before work and took a walk on the beach." She pointed toward the staff-only area behind the counter. "You could sit at my table. Andrea isn't due for a break for a while, so no one is using it."

I brightened. "Oh yeah, I'd forgotten about your secret garden."

She laughed again. "You're free to sit there. Just go through the back." She glanced at the round clock on the wall. "You know, I might join you." She added quickly, "If you don't mind the company, that is."

"I'd love for you to join me." Suddenly, chatting with a friend sounded like a much better option than sitting alone. I followed her behind the counter where she snagged a cup of coffee and a brownie for herself and then continued out the back door.

Recently, she'd made herself a small private sitting area outside, surrounded by white lattice work and colorful flowers. We sat down on the cushioned chairs and I leaned back for a moment, gazing up at the blue sky. "This is the life."

Desi sipped her coffee. "So, was Adam as bad as Tomàs about the packing? I swear, he threw a few things in a bag and called it good. I had to keep reminding him about things that he'd forgotten."

"What do you think?" I crushed a piece of brown sugar topping between my fingers. "And Adam thinks going tent camping would be fun. I can't imagine how much planning that would take for us and two little kids."

Desi scrunched up her face like she had tasted something sour.

"Yeah, that's going to be a while. I don't think I want to take the kids out tent camping at least until Lina is potty-trained. Tomàs and I made the mistake of taking Anthony camping when he was little, and let's just say it wasn't an enjoyable experience for either us or the people in the campsite next to us." She swigged the last drop of her coffee and stood, picking her plate up from the table. "I'm excited to see the resort after hearing you talk it up all these years."

I laughed. "I've never been there, so I hope it's all that Leah has made it seem."

"What made her move out there anyway?"

"I don't know. She got tired of the rat race, I guess." I wrapped my fingers around the handle of the cup. "If I hadn't left when I had kids, I probably would have reached the same point eventually. That commute was starting to wear on me."

"Was she always interested in the outdoors?"

An image of Leah in her high heels and tight pencil skirts flashed through my mind, making me laugh again.

"No. When I first met her, her idea of being outdoors was to have coffee on the rooftop deck of our building. But once she met Del, she started going hiking with him and I saw a gradual change in her. He brought out a whole new side of her that loved the outdoors." I shrugged. "After a while, being locked inside a building all day really got to her."

She nodded. "It would to me too. That's why I like being my own boss." She looked around. "Speaking of which, I'd better get back to work. We're pretty busy this morning, and I'm going to try to knock off around three so we can leave for the resort before rush hour."

I nodded. "I should get home too."

I finished my food and stood. Desi and I went back into the café and deposited our plates in the dishwashing sink. In the main part of the café, I heard a familiar voice talking to someone in line and I fought the urge to hunch down behind the counter.

Nancy Davenport. Any stress that had dissipated during my coffee chat with Desi came roaring back in full force. I contemplated going out the back way, but then steeled myself to walk past her.

"Hi, Nancy." I smiled, determined to kill her with kindness. I'd vowed that this year at preschool was going to be better than the last two. I had hoped that Nancy and I would have developed at least a cordial relationship by working together at the preschool auction last spring, but every interaction I had with her proved me wrong.

"Why hello, Jill. It's nice seeing you again. We didn't see much of you at the preschool after your parent volunteer week was up. Some of the parents come in every week, you know." She smiled at me with a cat-got-the-canary grin. "I was so sorry to hear that Mikey wasn't going to be attending Busy Bees Preschool in the upcoming school year."

I tilted my head to the side and gave her a quizzical look. "What do you mean, not attending? Mikey is going to be in the pre-K class this year."

She shook her head. "No, I don't think so. Danielle didn't receive a registration form for him, so he's not on the class list. The final deadline was last week."

I stared at her. Ice shot through my veins, pooling in my stomach. I closed my eyes briefly. In all the excitement of everything that had gone on over the summer and starting my new job, I'd completely spaced out on the registration deadline for Mikey's preschool.

"Will he be attending another preschool in Ericksville? I hear the one on Cherry Street is good," Nancy said, giving me a knowing smile.

I opened and closed my mouth like a fish. "You know, I have a registration form for Mikey, I'll just walk it over to Danielle today." I wasn't sure how I was going to manage to sandwich that into my already packed schedule before we left on our vacation, but I knew it needed to take priority over everything else. If Mikey didn't attend Busy Bees Preschool, I didn't think I'd be able to get him into another preschool or daycare on such short notice before school began in a little over a week.

She shook her head. "I'm sure Danielle has already given away his spot. The pre-K class is in high demand this year due to a bunch of parent referrals. Unfortunately, when she didn't receive his form by the registration date, you forfeited his spot in the class." The line moved and she shifted to the next place in the queue. My feet were frozen in place.

In a tight voice, I said, "Thank you for letting me know." I turned on my heels and walked quickly through the open door.

I paused outside of the café, my heart hammering in my chest. Mikey was going to kill me if he didn't end up at the same school as his cousin Anthony. The preschool's owner, Danielle, just had to let him in. I checked my watch. I really didn't have the time, but I decided to head over to the preschool before going back home. I hiked up the hill, stopping just before the front door.

The parking lot behind the school was empty. Chances were slim to none that Danielle was at work that day, as the preschool was closed for a few weeks before school started again. I crossed my fingers and took a deep breath, then pushed on the glass door. It was locked. I peered into the building, but the lights were out.

Nancy had compiled a handy school directory listing everyone's names and phone numbers, and I was pretty sure that Danielle's cell phone was listed on there. As soon as I got home, I'd give her a call to see if Nancy had been telling the truth about it being too late to register Mikey for preschool. This was not exactly how I'd pictured my morning going, but it seemed par for the course on a day where time was already at a premium.

When I got home, Adam and the kids were in the same place where I'd left them two hours before, although now they were snacking on Wheat Thins instead of toast. Mikey was still wearing his pajamas, and Ella had fallen asleep with her thumb in her mouth.

I needed to find that directory and call Danielle before I forgot about it.

"Adam, can you please get Mikey dressed? Has Ella been changed recently? We've got to get going." My rising stress levels made my words come out in a much harsher tone than I intended.

He turned around sharply and searched my face. "Are you ok?"

"I'm fine," I snapped. "I just have to find something." I rummaged through the files in my desk drawer, finally locating the directory. I ran my fingers over the names until I found Danielle's number. I carried the directory into another room and placed the phone call. Unfortunately, she didn't answer and I had to leave a message. My heart sank. Leah had warned me that the cell phone service at the resort was virtually nonexistent, and if I didn't hear from Danielle soon I might not know anything about Mikey's registration status until we returned home in a week. That was cutting it awfully close to the start of the school year.

Adam came up behind me and wrapped his arms around me, turning me to face him in the process. "Oh no," he said. "Were they out of coffee? I've never seen you this upset after coming back from the café."

His joke made me smile. "No. I had coffee." I squirmed a little then looked at him. "I forgot to register Mikey for Busy Bees and now he may not be able to attend."

He stepped back. "Oh. Is that a problem? Aren't there other daycares around?"

I looked at him with incredulity. "Most of them have a year-long wait-list. Besides, Mikey loves it there."

He leaned forward and kissed my forehead. "Don't worry, I'm sure things will work out. Can't you call them?"

I counted to ten slowly in my head. "I've already called the owner and left a message."

He shrugged. "Then you've done all you can. Now, let's get ready to leave. It's a long drive to Thunder Lake."

Some of Adam's calm must have rubbed off on me because I suddenly realized that he was right. I'd made a mistake, but I'd done the only thing I could do to fix it. Now I just needed to wait for Danielle to call me back. Everything would be ok, and I was sure she'd be reasonable about letting Mikey into the class. I kept repeating that to myself while I finished the packing and set everything by the garage door for Adam to load into the minivan.

While he installed the car-top carrier, I fixed myself and Adam iced coffees for the road and got the kids ready to leave.

He came in thirty minutes later, red-faced. "I hate that thing. It's so difficult to get on." He splashed water on his face. "And do we really need all that *stuff*?"

I fixed my eyes on him. "Yes."

He seemed to sense my heightened stress levels, because he just held his hands up in front of him and didn't mention again the car-top carrier or the *stuff* we were bringing with us. I herded Mikey out of the house and Adam carried Ella out. With any luck, we had remembered everything we would need.

Finally, we were settled in the car, ready to go. As Adam backed out of the driveway, I picked up my cell phone. It hadn't made any noise, but I'd hoped in the commotion of getting ready to leave, I'd missed a return call from Danielle.

Unfortunately, my screen was blank. Frustrated, I dropped it back into my purse. With any luck, she'd call back before our cell coverage dropped as we neared the resort. I leaned back in the passenger seat and gazed out the window as the sparkling waters of Puget Sound disappeared in the side-view mirrors.

3

"*M*ommy, how much longer until we get there?" Mikey whined. Between the captain's chairs in our minivan where he and his sister were seated, Goldie looked at me hopefully.

I gritted my teeth. "You asked me that two minutes ago. We've got about an hour to go." I consulted my map. "In fact, we should be getting to Pemberton pretty soon."

"We just passed a sign saying it was two miles away," Adam said, not taking his eyes off the road.

"Great." I turned back to Mikey. "Do you want to get a milkshake or something in Pemberton?"

His eyes grew as wide as plates. "Uh huh. Do they have strawberry?"

"I'm sure they do." I sat back in my seat and closed my eyes. It had been a very long four hours already since we'd left home.

"What's going on here?" Adam asked.

I opened my eyes and sat up. "What? Oh."

The main street through Pemberton was aglow with flashing red and blue lights.

"Something big must have happened. I'm kind of surprised they have more than one cop in this town." There were about five cop cars in front of the jewelry store.

Adam navigated around the police vehicles while Mikey and I craned our heads around to look at the commotion. What could have happened in a town this size to warrant such a response? Ella continued to sleep peacefully in her car seat, completely oblivious to everything going on around her.

"I see an ice cream cone!" Mikey shouted as he pointed eagerly to a shop on the corner.

"Where?" Adam asked. "I can't see anything in this sunshine." He shielded his eyes with one hand and drove right past the ice cream shop.

"Daddy! You missed it!"

"Well, I can't see a thing and those sirens are driving me nuts." Adam frowned. "Maybe we should just keep driving to the resort."

I put my hand on his shoulder and turned around to talk to Mikey. "Daddy's kidding. We'll turn around and go back." I eyed Adam. "Right?"

We'd passed the retail district of Pemberton and now were in a residential area. There wouldn't be any more ice cream shops down here.

He sighed but turned down the next block to head back to the main part of town.

"I see it. Turn right," I said. Adam complied and we parked a half block away from the ice cream sign.

We all got out of the car and stretched our legs. Even Ella woke up and yawned. I unclipped Goldie from his car restraint and attached his leash. He eagerly hopped out of the car and immediately began to sniff the flower beds along the curb.

The sun shone down on us, warming my face. The weather forecast had called for storms for the next few days, but I had to wonder if they'd been wrong. It definitely wouldn't be the first time. For now at least, the sky was a gorgeous light blue with not even a cloud in sight.

Mikey pranced in front of us as we made our way down the sidewalk to the place with the ice cream sign.

"Oh my gosh, this is so cute." I peered in the window while I waited for Adam to catch up. Ella was getting pretty heavy in her bucket seat, and I didn't think she'd be in it for much longer. I was glad Adam was carrying her and not me. I tied Goldie up outside near a doggy water dish.

"An old-fashioned ice cream parlor?" Adam pushed open the door with his hip. "I didn't think I'd ever see one of these again."

"Yeah, we used to go to one when I was a kid. They'd give us these huge sundaes on our birthday and all the employees would beat a drum and sing 'Happy Birthday.' I miss those days."

Mikey ran to the freezer full of ice cream at the front of the shop and pressed his face against the glass. I felt bad for the poor workers there who must have had to wash the case several times a day to get rid of all of the little kid nose prints.

We each chose our ice cream and dug in. Adam and I both got waffle cones and I felt like a kid again, crunching away on the sweet concoction. We took our treats outside to be with Goldie. The ice cream shop had installed an outdoor eating area, complete with a black and white checkered floor that made me feel like I'd been transported back in time. We sat in red padded chairs with white iron backs twisted into whimsical heart shapes.

A group of senior citizens went past us into the shop.

They placed their orders and then sat down with their ice cream at a larger table in the back corner of the outdoor patio. They were talking loudly enough that I couldn't help but eavesdrop.

"Do you think it was someone from around here who robbed the jewelry store?" asked a woman in her eighties sporting a cloud of puffy white hair.

"Nah, Arlene. It was probably some outsider." A man I presumed to be her husband took a bite of his Rocky Road ice cream. "Norbert Junell looked furious though. He was so proud of that new shipment of diamonds. Some rich person hired him to design a matching necklace and bracelet set. If he hadn't been bragging about them to everyone down at Rex's Place, they never would have robbed him of them."

"I don't know," the other woman with them said. "My son is on the police force and he said it didn't look like a professional job. Whoever stole the diamonds was lucky to get out of there without setting off the alarm. Apparently Norbert had forgotten to set it last night."

"He never was the brightest," the man said, swiping at a smear of chocolate ice cream on his face. "I remember him cheating off of me back in tenth grade math class."

"That was sixty years ago!" His wife shook her head. "You never forget anything."

"Nope," he said, with a self-satisfied grin on his face.

Adam nudged me. "Do you think we'll be like that in forty years?"

I laughed. "Probably."

"Oops," Mikey said, looking forlornly at the ground. "Sorry, Mommy."

I followed his eyes to the floor. "Mikey!"

He'd dropped half of his ice cream on the black and white tiles.

I took a deep breath. "It's ok. I'll get some napkins and clean it up." Adam handed me a handful of thin paper napkins from the dispenser on our table, but Goldie was quicker than we were and the mess was gone in one big gulp.

"I was getting full anyway." Mikey had chosen two scoops of ice cream, and I'd wondered if his eyes were bigger than his stomach.

"Don't worry about it." Adam put his hand on Mikey's shoulder. "I'm sure we'll have more ice cream on this trip. I intend to at least." He popped the remainder of his waffle cone in his mouth.

Mikey brightened. "Yeah! Next time I'm getting Bubble Gum ice cream for my first scoop and peanut butter for my second scoop."

I gagged at the combination but didn't say anything. Mikey finished what was left of his ice cream cone, and I walked past the senior citizens to throw away the soiled napkins.

They were still talking about the jewelry store robbery, although now they spoke in hushed voices, so I couldn't make out much of what they were saying. It must have been big news in this small town.

When we were back in the car and waiting for Mikey to get himself situated in his car seat, Adam glanced over at me.

"Well, that was some excitement. Who'd have thought this sleepy little town would be the scene of a big jewel heist?"

I laughed. "I'm hoping that's all the excitement we get. I have big plans for relaxing by the lake." I pictured myself kicking back in one of the Adirondack chairs I'd seen in the advertisements for the resort, drinking a cup of coffee and enjoying a warm breeze ruffling my hair.

He smiled. "Somehow I don't think this is going to be as relaxing as our couples only vacation back in June. Remember that romantic dinner we had on the beach?"

I closed my eyes for a moment, remembering the warmth of the Jamaican sun on my face and the most amazing meal I'd ever had. I glanced at the back seat. Mikey was wriggling around like he had ants in his pants, and Ella looked like she was about to cry.

I climbed into the van to help Mikey get buckled then turned back to Adam. "Probably not."

"There it is, the Thunder Lake Resort." I pointed at the sign, and Adam made a sharp left onto a gravel road that wound through a heavily forested area.

When we got closer, the lake came into view, the blue waters glittering in the sun. Tall hills rose above the wooded shores. There ought to be plenty of hiking trails here for Adam.

"Whoa," Mikey said, craning his neck around his car seat to lean out over the middle and see out the windshield of our minivan. "It's so big."

I laughed. The lake wasn't huge, but to a four-year-old, it was probably humongous. I stared out at the lake and a shiver ran through me. Thunder Lake was about the same size as Lake Elinor, where a maniac had tried to drown Desi and me a month ago. I hoped I'd have better memories of this lake.

We rounded a corner and drove under a wooden sign

with the name of the resort carved into it. Adam parked the car in front of a general store-type building, which I assumed was the office. Sure enough, hidden behind a hanging pot of giant impatiens was a small sign with "Office" printed on it.

Adam turned the car off and glanced around. "It's bigger than I thought it would be."

I nodded. I hadn't known what to expect either. When Leah and Del bought the place, it hadn't been in the best condition. Now, all of the cabins were freshly painted forest green with charming white accent paint. A few of them were lined up alongside the lakefront and had decks overlooking the water. A sense of calm came over me. We hadn't been on a family vacation since Mikey was one, and I was going to make the most of spending quality time with my family.

"I'll go into the office and register. You stay with the kids."

"Fine with me. I'm tired." He released his seat belt and leaned back against the headrest. "It's been a long drive."

I glanced at the bags of chips and candy wrappers littering the front of the car. "Well, we would have been here an hour ago if we hadn't stopped every two hours for food."

"We needed provisions." He mock glared at me. "Now go, I'm going to catch a minute of shut-eye here if I can."

I checked the back seat. Mikey's eyes were glued to the lake, probably contemplating which of the boats he wanted to take out, and Ella was fast asleep in her car seat.

"Ok, I'll be back soon."

I got out of the car and stretched my legs. Adam was right—it had been a long ride from the Seattle area to the northeastern corner of Washington State. But it had been worth it. Overhead, birds chirped from perches high up in the trees and sunlight filtered through the pine branches. According to the thermometer in our car, the temperature in this part of the state was hovering in the high seventies. Everything about this place signaled rest and relaxation, from the canoes floating lazily on the water, down to the rough-hewn log benches on the wide front porch of the building in front of me.

I pushed open the door to the office and stepped back in time. Wooden floors creaked under my feet as I passed shelves of everything a person could need at a lake resort—inner tubes, fishing gear, s'mores fixings, and much more. There was a reason they called general stores—they had a little of everything in them.

Leah stood behind the counter, talking to an elderly couple with matching white hair. They thanked her and left.

Leah's face lit up when she saw me. "Jill! I'm so glad you're here." She came around the counter and gave me a big hug.

I returned the hug and then stepped back to take a look at her. While she'd been skinny when she'd worked with me back in Seattle, here she'd developed a more muscular structure and she glowed with health. "You look great," I said.

"Thanks." She smiled at me. "There's something about being around nature that I seem to respond to. I never thought of myself as much of an outdoorsy person, but I love it here." She beamed as she surveyed her store and the lake through the window.

"Well, you have a lot to be proud of. I remember you showing me pictures of the place when you and Del were considering buying it." I waved my hand at the cabins, off in the distance. "You guys must have put a lot of work into making this what it is today." I hugged her again. "I'm so excited to be here. I know my family is going to love this place."

"I hope so. We've done everything we can to make this place a success." Her expression clouded over for a second, and then a bright smile replaced it. I wasn't sure if I'd imagined it because she said, "We've been booked solid for the last couple of months. If we can get some business in the winter, we'll be set."

"I'm sure things will work out." I wandered over to the window. "Which of the cabins are we going to be in? Will my sister-in-law's cabin be close to ours?"

She snapped her fingers and laughed. "In my excitement about seeing you again, I almost forgot you are a guest here." She motioned for me to come to the counter and she went behind it and tapped away at the computer. "I've got you in cabins next to each other along the lake. Does that work for you? It's a little further away from the café and recreation areas, but most people think being right on the lake completely makes up for the slightly longer walk."

"That's perfect." I could already see myself sipping coffee out on the deck. Maybe I could even convince Adam to take the kids for a while, and I could take a nap on the nylon rope hammock that I had spied hanging off to one side of the decks.

Leah registered us and held out two keys for the cabin and a pamphlet detailing the activities at the resort. "We have s'mores out at the campfire at eight o'clock every night, and then a pancake breakfast in the morning. Of course, if you want espresso, the café opens at six a.m. It's in the Great Hall, directly behind the office." She laughed. "I seem to remember you having a raging caffeine addiction."

I smiled. "I still do. It may even be worse now with having two kids who don't often sleep through the night." I took the keys from her and she led me outside.

"I'm going to be pretty busy tonight checking people in,

but stop by and see me tomorrow. If I'm not here, that's my house up there." She pointed to a two-story log cabin at the edge of the woods. "Feel free to come see me when you can. I'd love to catch up on everything." She shook her head. "It's hard to believe you have two kids already. It seems like yesterday that we were hanging out after work."

"It's hard for me to believe sometimes too." Going back to work at the Boathouse had been good for me, but I was still trying to figure out who I was again after having my kids.

"Anyway, you're in cabin six. It's right over there." She nodded at the lakefront cabins I'd seen before. "Your sister-in-law will be in cabin five. Do you know when she'll be checking in?"

"I don't think she'll be here until nine or ten tonight. Is that ok? Will there be someone to check her in?"

"Of course. I'll make sure everything is arranged." Leah rested her hand on my arm. "I've got to get back to work, but don't forget to come catch up with me later."

"I will," I called over my shoulder. I walked quickly to the car, dangling the keys in front of me. When I opened the car door, Adam was still snoozing in the front seat, but Mikey looked excited to see me. I sat down and turned around in the front passenger seat to see him better.

"Can we go out canoeing now? Or maybe exploring in the woods? I hope there are bears here. I want to see a bear. Anthony will want to go too."

Bears? I hoped there weren't any around the resort. I glanced at the thick woods on the outskirts of the property. There probably were a plethora of forest creatures living in them. I shuddered. Probably mice and other little rodents. Maybe I'd send Adam out alone with Mikey on a hike.

I put my hand on Adam's shoulder and shook it. "Wake up."

"Huh, what?" His eyes flashed open and he put his hands on the steering wheel. "Where are we?"

I sighed. Adam had always been a deep sleeper, and it often took him a few minutes and a gallon of coffee to wake up.

"We're at the Thunder Lake Resort. I talked to Leah and I've got our cabin assignment. It's right over there—cabin six." I nodded my head toward the cabins.

"Oh." He focused his attention on the cabins. "Great." He inserted the key in the ignition and started the car, then slowly drove over to cabin six. We parked in one of the two spots in front of the cabin, our tires stopping softly on a bed of dried pine needles.

Ella had awoken, and Adam removed her from her carrier and held her against his chest as I unbuckled Mikey. As soon as he was free, our son bounded from the car and up the steps to the cabin. He raced around the covered deck to the water side.

"Hey, wait up." I jogged after him. We'd been trying to teach him how to swim, but he hadn't mastered the skill yet and I didn't want him falling in. When I got to him, he was clutching the railing and staring out at the water.

"This is going to be so cool!"

"Yep." I took his hand and led him over to the door. The key turned easily and we were in the cabin. The inside was rustic, but nicely kept up, with a couch out in the living room, one bedroom with a queen-size bed, and a smaller room with twin-sized bunk beds. An even smaller bathroom was tucked away behind a galley kitchen. The living room contained a fireplace with a huge rag rug in front of it. I didn't think we'd have much need for the fireplace on our trip, but it would be nice for a winter visit.

It wasn't glamorous, but it was one hundred times nicer than roughing it in the woods like Adam had wanted to do. I planned to put Ella in the Pack 'n Play we'd brought with us for her to sleep in, and Mikey would sleep in the bottom bunk.

Adam came in and handed Ella to me. "I'll bring our bags in."

Mikey explored the cabin. "Hey, where's the TV?" He opened a cabinet under the kitchen sink, as if hoping it would be there.

"There isn't one." I smiled sweetly at him, taking secret pleasure in his disappointment. "We're not here to watch TV. We do enough of that at home."

"I guess." He didn't look convinced.

I checked my cell phone, but there was no signal. If Danielle had called back, I wouldn't be getting her message anytime soon. I guess Mommy was off of her electronics for the week too. It would be refreshing to let go of things in the outside world for a while, right?

Adam reappeared with our two bags, then went back for the rest of our stuff. Ella's bouncer came in followed by the bin I'd used to corral the sippy cups, bottles, and other baby supplies we'd require for a week's stay. Back in the days of being a dual-income childless couple, we'd been able to hop on a plane with only our carry-ons. Those days were long gone.

Mikey tugged on my arm. "Can I go outside now?"

"Uh." I looked at Adam. Ella squirmed in my arms and wailed loudly. "Sorry, Mikey, I think I need to feed your sister."

"She's always eating." He pouted and glared at Ella.

"Why don't you and Daddy go for a walk or something? Oh, and I saw a playground on the way over here."

"Yeah!" Mikey turned to Adam. "I want to go to a playground!"

Adam grinned and ruffled his hair. "Let's go."

4

*a*fter they left, I brought Ella into the back bedroom of the cabin to give her a bottle and enjoy the temporary quiet. I sat down with her on the cheery flowered comforter, the mattress springs squeaking under my weight. She hungrily sucked down the bottle and then her eyes drooped. After she fell asleep, I propped her up in the middle of the queen-sized bed on her Boppy and crossed the room to grab a book out of my suitcase. Before I reached the other side of the room, angry voices floated into the room through the open window. One of them sounded like Leah.

The curtain danced in the soft breeze, enticing me to see what was going on. I pulled back the soft cotton fabric and peered out the small screened window.

I'd been right. Leah and a man I recognized as Del were standing next to an oak tree about twenty feet away from our cabin.

"You've got to be kidding me. Someone broke all of the bows and arrows at the archery range?" Leah gestured wildly with her hands. "We can't afford to replace all of those."

"I know. We've got to find out who's doing this." Del ran his fingers through his short brown hair.

"I just don't understand why someone is doing this to the resort. I thought at first that it was a malicious guest or something, but it's gone on for too long. It has to be someone from the area—or someone who works here."

Del sighed. "I know, but even if it is, I don't know what you want me to do about it. We reported the other incidents to the police, but they just don't have the manpower to investigate petty crimes like this."

"Well, they should." Leah jutted out her chin. "This is costing us money. And you're in charge of the grounds. If you can't get the police to do their job, it's your responsibility to figure out who is vandalizing our property."

"You're the one who wants to keep this resort. You need to take some responsibility too." He stared defiantly at her.

"I feel like you don't understand how severe this could be. When someone sawed partially through the leg of that bench and it collapsed under a guest, they could have been badly hurt. We were lucky they only had some cuts and bruises. If they'd sued us, that would be the end of the resort." She turned to look past the row of cabins to the lake.

I ducked down, then inched my way back up and peered at them through a crack in the curtains.

Leah uttered a harsh laugh. "And if the vandalism wasn't enough, your cousin hasn't fixed the railing on the end of the dock yet. That thing is coming loose and we're going to have some kid fall in the lake when it goes."

"The railing isn't as bad as you're making it out to be, and it's on his list," Del said in a tight voice. "Jed gets his work done."

"I don't see how, he's a lazy bum who disappears during the middle of the day." She folded her arms across her chest. "I can never find him when I need something fixed. Isn't that why we let him come here?"

"I'm not talking about this anymore." Del turned on his heels and stalked away, leaving Leah standing there just watching him.

She swiped at her face with the back of her hands. I was too far away to see the tears, but I could tell from her expression that she was crying.

My heart hurt for my old friends. Something was obviously amiss with their relationship. Was this the cause of Leah's brief moment of sadness earlier? When I'd known them years ago, they'd been so in love. Before I'd met Adam, I'd wished for what they had. When they'd moved to the lake, they'd been so full of hopes and dreams for their future together. How had things gone so wrong?

Whatever what going on between them, I needed to remember that my main focus was my family. I wasn't going to let anything ruin our vacation together.

The screen door to our cabin squeaked and Mikey's eager voice bubbled into the bedroom. I cast a glance at Ella, who was still asleep on the bed, and joined Mikey and Adam in the main room of our cabin.

When he was finished setting up Ella's bed, Adam looked at me. "Now what?"

I found the pamphlet Leah had given me. "We could go canoeing, hiking, play horseshoes, or even go fishing. I think they sell fishing licenses here."

He brightened. "It's been a while since I've been lake

fishing. I bet Tomàs would love to go too when they get here."

"Probably." This would be good for the two guys to bond a little. With Adam's busy work schedule as a lawyer and Tomàs's as a police officer, they hadn't spent much time together, even though Desi and Tomàs had been married for close to ten years. We saw each other at family events, and Desi and I were best friends now, but our families hadn't ever spent significant amounts of time together. With any luck, we wouldn't want to kill each other by the time the week was over.

Adam and I finally agreed on a rousing game of horse-shoes, followed by dinner at the café. Stuffed with lake trout, we relaxed on the deck until it was time for s'mores. We left Goldie behind in the cabin and dressed the kids in their jackets for an evening outside. I didn't think Mikey had ever eaten a s'more, so I wondered if he'd like it or not. Then I realized how stupid that was. Of course he would like it, it was a sugar sandwich.

The sky had darkened, but we could see the glow of the communal fire pit behind our row of cabins. Other vaca-tioners had gathered around its warmth, their faces illumi-nated by the flames. I held Ella tight against me and searched for a log to sit on. A teenager offered me their seat after being nudged to do so by their parents. I gratefully accepted. Might as well take advantage of one of the perks that came along with parenthood.

Adam took Mikey over to the opposite side of the giant fire pit and handed him a long wooden roasting stick topped by a fresh marshmallow. Mikey proceeded to stick it into the coals. When he pulled it out, it resembled a tiki torch. Adam blew out the flames and threw the charcoaled marshmallow into the fire. This time, he helped Mikey hold it over the cooler coals near the edge. I laughed, remembering my own marshmallow mishaps and the sticks my father had carved for us when we'd go on camping trips. This time though, I didn't eat any s'mores myself, choosing instead to simply enjoy the warmth of the fire on my face. On my lap, Ella looked on with interest as strangers chatted around her.

After enjoying a s'more, Mikey and Adam came back over to us. The crowd had thinned and they were able to sit next to me on the log. Mikey waved the sharp stick around and I winced. The wooden stick didn't look quite as lethal as the metal ones some people had, but I still worried about the safety of it.

"Honey, put that down. You could poke someone's eye out with it."

"No I won't, Mom!" He waved it around some more. A terrifying image of someone being impaled on one of the sticks floated into my mind. Being a mom, I had a tendency to imagine the worst possible scenario in every situation.

Adam sighed. "He's fine." However, I noticed that he removed it from Mikey's hands and placed it with the others on top of a large rock.

Mikey yawned and his eyes drooped.

"I think it's time for bed," Adam observed. Mikey started to lean over on the log, and Adam caught him before he toppled to the ground. Mikey snuggled against Adam, who picked him up to walk the short distance back to our cabin. I followed close behind with Ella.

When the kids were snugly tucked in their beds, I opened the window in the bedroom a crack to allow fresh air to enter, then crept under the covers of the bigger bed I shared with Adam. He was already snoring away next to me, but I lay there for a few minutes, smelling the scent of pine trees and the faint odor of campfire smoke. It reminded me of camping with my parents when I was a kid.

Growing up nearby in Idaho, we'd often camp in this part of Washington, usually near a lake or river where my dad would take us fishing. I swallowed a lump in my throat, thinking about my parents. They'd separated in early summer, but neither of them had moved out of their house, so I maintained a child-like fantasy that they'd eventually reconcile. Whatever happened between them, I'd always have the wonderful memories of times we spent together as a family. I hoped Mikey would have many happy memories of this trip with his family, just as I had of mine.

The next morning, I awoke to things much like they'd been the night before. The kids and Adam were sleeping soundly, but my mind was wide awake. The sun shone through a gap in the curtains and I eased out of bed, careful not to wake anyone up. I didn't feel like fiddling around with the boxes of food we'd brought to find the ground coffee. I glanced down at the yoga pants and tank top that I'd slept in. Probably fine for a quick trip to the café for a morning espresso.

I stretched and moved toward the front door, apparently signaling to Goldie that it was time for a walk. He appeared next to me, ready to go and not taking no for an answer. I sighed and clipped a leash onto his harness to take him with me, then opened the door.

Immediately, the rays of the early morning sun and the scent of the fresh outdoor air embraced me. There still wasn't any sign that the weather was about to change, and I crossed my fingers that it would stay sunny for our entire vacation. I eyed the cute wrought iron bistro table in one corner of the deck. It was calling my name—all I needed was a nice cup of coffee.

Next door, Desi's minivan was parked in front of cabin number five. They must have arrived after we'd gone to bed, admittedly earlier than we usually retired for the evening. If they were awake, maybe she and Tomàs would like coffee too.

I listened for a moment to see if they were up but didn't hear anything, so I hiked up the hill away from the lake, toward the campfire pit above our line of cabins. In the light of day, the fire pit looked even bigger than it had last night, full of the charcoaled remains of the giant logs that had been burned the night before.

I rounded the corner, near the fake stone cabinet the resort must use for storage, and stopped in my tracks. Goldie barked loudly, and I pulled him closer while I focused on the sight in front of me. Behind the cabinet, partially concealed by the log I'd sat on last night, was a person, lying on the ground.

My heart almost stopped and I froze for a moment. This was too close to the time I'd found Mr. Westen's body next to a beach log last spring. He'd clearly been dead, but that didn't mean this person was too.

Get a grip, Jill. It's probably someone taking a nap out in the great outdoors.

The thought struck me as ridiculous. Why would someone be sleeping out here on the gravel surrounding a campfire pit when they could have stretched out in the grass nearby? Even so, I approached the man, hoping against hope that this time the person in question was still alive.

"Hey, are you ok?" I asked.

The closer I got, the more certain I was that this man

was definitely not ok. As I'd imagined in my silly fears last night, he'd been impaled by one of the metal roasting sticks that were piled into the half-open cabinet. His face was white and lifeless, his hands outstretched toward the grass surrounding the pit.

5

$\mathcal{I}$ shrieked and stared wide-eyed at the body. After further examination of his face, I sighed in relief. I didn't recognize the man, but as we'd only arrived yesterday evening, that didn't mean much.

"What's going on?" Desi called out from behind me. "I heard Goldie barking and then you screamed. Are you ok?"

I whipped around and pointed to the ground in front of me. She came around to my side of the fire pit, clutching Lina to her chest. She wore a tank top and shorts and shivered in the shade of a pine tree.

Her eyes widened. "Who is that?"

"I don't know, but I'm pretty sure he's dead."

"Yeah, no kidding." Oddly enough, she didn't seem surprised by the appearance of a dead body on our first morning at the resort.

"We have to tell someone." She stared at him too. "I can't leave the area." She pointed at their cabin. "Anthony's asleep, and I don't want to leave him alone."

"I'll go see if anyone is in the office." I turned to leave

then spun back around. Something she'd said seemed strange. "Where's Tomàs? Can't he watch Anthony?"

She shrugged. "He's coming up in a few days. There's been a bug going around the police station and they're short-staffed, so he volunteered to take a few more shifts."

"I kind of wish he was here. That doesn't look like a natural death." As much as I'd wanted to have this be a peaceful family vacation, things weren't looking good for that to happen.

She glanced over to the body again too. "No."

"I'm not sure how long this will take. If Adam comes out looking for me, can you tell him I went to the office?"

She nodded. "Go."

I scurried off to the office with Goldie in tow, but no one was there yet. I knew the café opened at six, so I headed over there next. There weren't any other customers, but Leah was busy behind the counter, making a pot of drip coffee.

She smiled at me. "Hey, I didn't expect to see you up this early. It's a beautiful day though, isn't it?" Her voice was as chirpy as the birds in the trees outside.

I took a deep breath. "I have some upsetting news."

Leah cocked her head to the side. "What is it? Did something happen with your cabin? Sometimes the toilet in that one can be a little tricky."

"No, the toilet is fine." I glanced out the window. "There's been an accident." I was pretty sure it wasn't an accident, but I wasn't sure if she knew the victim and I wanted to soften the news.

"What? Is everyone all right?" She came out from behind the counter to stand next to me. Behind her, the coffee percolated loudly into the pot.

I pressed my lips together. "No. There's a man's body by the fire pit. He's dead."

Her eyes widened. "Oh, my goodness, that's horrible. Are you sure he's dead? Was it a heart attack? Maybe we can do CPR." She started to rush out the door, but I stopped her.

"I'm sorry, Leah, but he's gone. There's nothing you can do."

"But how do you know?" Her eyes darted wildly toward the direction of the fire pit. "Wait, is it Del?" Terror streaked through her voice.

"No, it's not Del. I don't recognize the man. I think you should call the authorities though. I don't think this was a natural death."

"What do you mean?" Fear crossed her face.

She was going to see it soon enough. "C'mon, I'll show you. You probably should bring a sheet or something. You're not going to want to let the other guests see this."

Leah called the police and they promised her they'd be there within ten minutes. Her face was as white as the sheet she'd grabbed out of the back room before we walked at a brisk pace toward the campfire. Desi stood near the campfire pit, away from the body and keeping an eye on her cabin.

"I wanted to make sure no one else disturbed the scene." She glanced at the sheet. "Do you think you should put that over him? I mean, what if it changes the evidence or something?"

I looked at her. Ever the wife of a policeman, Desi had a point.

While we were discussing the sheet, Leah had moved closer to the body. If possible, her face had paled in comparison to what it had looked like a few minutes earlier. She seemed to recognize the deceased.

"Do you know him?" I asked her.

39

She nodded, tears slipping from her eyes. "That's Del's cousin, Jed."

"Oh no." Poor Del. I didn't know what to say. Now that she mentioned it though, I could see the resemblance between Del and Jed.

"Why would someone do that to him?" Her eyes kept darting to the marshmallow roasting stick embedded in Jed's body. "I don't understand."

The gentle breeze I'd felt this morning had become stronger, bringing with it the acrid odor of last night's fire. I put my arm around her shoulders and turned her away from the campfire pit. I whispered over my shoulder to Desi, "Keep an eye on the scene, ok?"

Desi nodded. I moved Leah over to a tree nearby and we waited there, huddled together until the authorities arrived. Soon, the campground was awash in flashing red, blue, and white lights as an ambulance and police cars circled the area. A crowd gathered as the commotion attracted them. By this time, Desi had retrieved Anthony from their cabin, and Adam had taken both boys and Goldie down to the lake. We hoped to distract them from what had happened only a few hundred feet from where they'd been sleeping, but there was nothing we could do to erase that knowledge from our own brains.

The police surrounded Leah, asking her questions about Jed. Her face was devoid of any emotion by this point.

A beat-up red truck spewing dark clouds of smelly exhaust pulled up to the office and a man jumped out— Del. Leah saw him coming and broke away from the police.

She ran to him and hugged him, then said something to him, presumably breaking the bad news about his cousin.

Desi nudged me and whispered, "He looks just like the

dead guy. Leah must have been scared that it was Del before she was close enough to tell it wasn't."

I nodded. "I know. I didn't notice how much he looked like Del when I discovered the body, but in my defense, it was early and I wasn't caffeinated yet."

We watched as Del's face turned ashen. He walked toward the police but didn't stop until he'd reached the campfire pit. The police had finished assessing the scene and had laid a sheet over the body while they spoke to possible witnesses. Leah trailed after him.

"Is that Jed?" Del shakily pointed a finger at the body. The sheet over Jed flapped in the wind, leaving only the roasting stick visible where it protruded from under the white cloth.

One of the policemen stepped forward to address him. "Did you know the deceased, sir?"

Del nodded. "Leah," he nodded at her, "said it's Jed, my cousin." He shook his head. "But what could have happened to him? I don't understand."

The policeman wrote some notes on his pad. "We're going to need to talk to you about your cousin. Maybe you'd be more comfortable over there at the picnic table." He gestured to a nearby table.

Del trembled as he considered the offer, his eyes still glued to the sheet-covered body. "Ok."

They walked over to the table, out of earshot. The police seemed to be done with Leah, so Desi and I stood with her off to the side.

"I'm so sorry, Leah," Desi said. "This is awful."

Leah wiped away a tear. "I can't believe it. I just saw him yesterday."

"Were you close to Jed?" I asked, handing her a Kleenex from the box I'd stolen from our cabin.

"Close enough, I guess. We didn't always get along, but he and Del were like brothers. We didn't see him much until we bought the resort. Then, he moved out here from the Midwest to help us out." She shrugged. "I'm not sure he had much going on out there."

"Is there anyone else you should notify?"

She shook her head. "No. Neither of them had any other living relatives. That's part of the reason they're so close."

We were all quiet as the police finished their investigation and the body was loaded onto an ambulance, which then slowly drove away without its customary flashing lights. With all of the emergency personnel gone, the crowd surrounding the fire pit dispersed. Leah left to go man the store and Adam came back with the boys. We walked with the kids over to the nearby playground.

Desi, Adam, and I sat in awkward silence as we watched the boys swing. This trip was becoming much more than we'd bargained for. Finally, I voiced what we'd all been thinking.

"Should we go home?"

6

---

a gray cloud had moved over the lake, dropping the temperature by twenty degrees. I shivered and hugged my arms to my chest. I was still wearing the yoga pants and tank top I'd worn to bed the night before.

I glanced at the boys, now racing around the playground. Wood chips shot out behind their feet as they ran. They were so happy and we'd all been looking forward to this trip for so long. I turned my gaze to the fire pit. Someone had been skulking around behind our cabins last night, murdering Del's cousin. I shivered again, and not from the cold.

"What do you think?" I asked Adam.

His eyes were troubled. "I don't know. It worries me to have a murderer on the loose. Even though it probably was an isolated incident, I'm not sure I can get over that."

Desi shifted her weight on her feet and traced circles in the dusty ground with the tip of her sneaker. "I don't think Tomàs would like this very much." She looked at me. "I'm sorry, Jill, but I think we're out. I'll call him and let him know not to come up here."

43

A drop of rain hit Desi's forehead and her gaze shot up to the sky. "Ugh, this doesn't look good. I think it's going to dump on us at any minute."

Adam and I looked upward. The sky over the lake and resort had darkened into a field of ominous rain clouds. Every bit of our sunny day had disappeared, just as the weatherman had predicted.

Suddenly, the sky opened up and fat drops of rain pelted us. Desi covered Lina's head in her front carrier and Adam moved the stroller's shade over Ella.

I cupped my hands like a megaphone. "Boys, we've got to go inside."

They continued playing, seemingly oblivious to the rain and wind.

"Go get the babies inside," I shouted to Adam and Desi as a strong gust whipped through the campground, blowing strands of my long hair into my face. "I'll get the kids."

They nodded and hurried toward the cabins. I ran over to the playset and called up into it from a slide entrance.

"Mikey, Anthony! We've got to get inside before we get soaked."

They came over to me, but still clung to the wooden play structure.

"Why, Auntie Jill?" Anthony asked.

"Yeah, we want to play longer," Mikey whined.

I gave them an incredulous look and pointed up at the sky, getting my face wet in the process. "Do you really not see the rain?"

Mikey shrugged. "It's always raining back home."

I sighed and grabbed their hands. He was right—another reason I'd hoped for a nice sunny vacation before the dreary Pacific Northwest winter set in. "Let's go."

They reluctantly followed me back to the covered deck

of our cabin. Desi and Adam stood there, peering at the lake. While it had been a beautiful sheet of glass this morning, it was now a frenzy of whitecaps. I hoped no fishermen or boaters had been caught out there when the storm hit.

"What now?" I asked. "Desi, are you going to go to the pay phone to call Tomàs?"

"Not right now. Are you crazy? I'd be drenched after only one foot away from the cabin. I'll call him as soon as the rain lets up."

Adam looked at me. "Did you decide whether or not to stay?"

I wiped a lock of dripping hair away from my forehead and leaned against the wall. "I don't know. I almost feel like I should stay. Leah doesn't have much family out here, so she could use my support. I didn't know Jed, but I doubt this was a random attack. The person who killed him is probably long gone."

Adam pressed his lips together, then sighed. "I don't know."

"How about we give it a few hours to think about it? By then, the storm should have died down and we can talk about it some more." I gestured to the board games we'd brought with us. "We could play Sorry or Uno? Maybe even Candy Land?"

Desi glanced at Lina, who was now sleeping soundly on a pile of pillows in the corner. Ella had also fallen asleep in her Pack 'n Play. She shrugged. "Works for me."

I clapped my hands. "Boys, we're going to play a game." I pointed at the colorful rag rug that covered the floor of our cabin's living area. "Sit."

They dutifully sat and we adults eased ourselves onto the floor as well.

"I'm getting too old to sit on the floor," Adam grumbled.

Next to him, Desi laughed. "Yep. You're pretty ancient, big brother."

He gave her a gentle shove and glared at her, causing her to giggle and pretend to fall to the floor.

A warmth came over me. With how strained the first full day of our vacation had already been, it was nice to see a touch of normalcy.

~

After two games of Uno, one of Sorry, and a simple lunch of deli meat sandwiches with baby carrots, the rain had finally let up, although the skies were still gray.

Desi stood and stretched. "I'd better call Tomàs now and let him know not to come."

She sounded disappointed. We'd been cocooned in the cabin for hours, and it felt like ages ago that I'd discovered a body at the fire pit. The three of us adults moved toward the cabin's door, leaving the boys to squirm around like worms on the thick carpet.

"Are you sure you want to leave?" I asked, watching her closely.

Her eyes flitted to the lake. "I really wanted—no," she corrected herself, "needed this vacation, but I don't know what Tomàs will think. I'm going to call him and ask him what he wants to do. He has more experience in this type of thing than I do."

I nodded. Tomàs had been on the Ericksville police force for over ten years and he was level-headed in most matters. I trusted his opinion.

Adam and I exchanged glances.

"I'm inclined to go with what Tomàs thinks," Adam said to Desi. His eyes flickered to me. "Jill, is that ok with you?"

"Yes." I checked on the boys. Mikey was teaching Anthony how to do a somersault. "If Tomàs thinks we should leave, we'll leave too."

In a relieved voice, Desi said, "Great. Then it's settled. I'll go over to the office and call him to see what he thinks. Can you watch Lina and Anthony for me?" She peered out the window. "I think the rain has mainly stopped, but I don't want them to get cold out there."

"Of course." I smiled at her. "Lina's asleep anyway and I don't think we'll be able to pry Anthony away from Mikey any time soon."

Over on the rug, Anthony and Mikey giggled as they pretended to be dogs, barking at each other.

Desi grabbed her sweatshirt from where it hung in front of the fireplace. "I'll be back as soon as I can."

As soon as she left, I turned to Adam. "I really don't want to leave. We made the reservations for this vacation a year ago. It's our first since Mikey was a baby."

He pulled me close against him and I laid my head on his chest.

"I know. But we don't want to be here if it's not safe." He rested his chin on the top of my head.

"I know." My heart felt heavy. I didn't want to go back home when we should be having fun out on the lake. It wasn't fair.

He stepped back and looked into my eyes. "We'll see what Tomàs says, ok?"

"Ok." Being cooped up in the cabin was making me squirrely. "Do you mind watching all the kids for a few minutes? I'd love to take a short walk."

"Sure. No problem." He hugged me again. "Don't worry, honey, it will all work out. If we can't stay here, maybe we can find a camping spot instead." He eyed me hopefully.

"Maybe." I was happy to agree because I knew there was absolutely zero chance of any camping spots being available for Labor Day weekend.

I plucked a sweatshirt out of my suitcase and stepped outside the cabin. The air smelled like fresh rain, and the clouds swirling above us hinted that the first squall passing through wouldn't be the last. I intended to walk down toward the lake, but instead, my feet took me up the hill to the fire pit.

The circle of logs was empty and only the disturbed dirt and gravel where the body had been lying hinted at what had happened earlier in the day.

An image of the body flashed into my brain. He'd been sprawled on his side, speared in the back by the marsh-mallow stick. I shuddered. I knew those things were dangerous.

Had Jed even known there was somebody else out there? Why had he been at the fire pit in the first place?

I shook my head. Unlike the murder investigations I'd been dragged into in the past, this one didn't directly affect me. The soft tapping of footsteps behind me made me whirl around.

"Whoa." Desi held up her hands. "It's just me." She glanced at the fire pit. "Why are you up here?"

I laughed self-consciously. "I don't know." What was I doing here?

"Something about murder scenes just draws you to them?" she asked dryly.

"Yeah, something like that." I peered at her. "What did Tomàs say?" I crossed my fingers that he would say it was perfectly fine for us to stay at the resort.

She sighed. "The phone lines are down. I couldn't call him."

"Really? I'm surprised the power isn't out too. Back home the electricity and phones usually go out together."

She shrugged. "I don't know. Leah says it's pretty common around here. Something about the phone lines being overhead, but the rest of the utilities being underground. She said I could use the internet in the office to e-mail him, but he never checks his personal e-mail account." She sighed deeply. "Anyway, if I want to call Tomàs, I'll need to drive back to Pemberton."

"But that's over an hour away." I checked the sky, not surprised to find that it was still gray and scary. At least it wasn't raining at the moment.

"I know. And those roads weren't fun in good conditions. I don't want to try to navigate them in the rain and worry about trees crashing down on my car."

"So, what are you going to do?" I asked.

"I don't know. Hopefully, this storm will clear up and if the phone lines are still out, I can drive into town tomorrow before Tomàs leaves our house. I'd hate for him to drive all the way out here and then have to turn right back around."

I nodded. "Sounds like a good plan."

"What do we do now though?" Desi waved her hands around in a wide half circle. "Swimming's out and so is hiking. I can't imagine being stuck in a cabin with the boys for the rest of the day."

"Well, obviously we won't be roasting s'mores tonight."

She slugged me in the arm. "Too soon."

"Ow. I just meant because of the rain," I said lamely, rubbing the sore spot. "What do you think about dinner at the café? I've heard the fish and chips there are good. The trout we had last night was amazing."

She shrugged. "I guess so. Beats the cans of veggie beef stew I brought."

49

We gathered the rest of our family and ran with the stroller through the rainstorm to the small café located in the Great Hall. On the covered deck, we shook the rain off of our jackets and the hood of Lina's stroller and pushed open the door to the large hall. Apple-cinnamon aromas filled the air and a glass baked goods shelf displayed the pies available for the night. I wasn't sure we'd have a chance to get any of the delicious smelling Dutch apple pie though, because apparently, we hadn't been the only family with the idea to eat out for dinner. A line had formed all the way out to the recreation hall.

"I'll stand in line here if you want to take the kids to play in there." Adam nodded at the game room.

Desi and I looked at each other. "Sure," I said.

We entered an impressive recreation hall. Teenagers were playing pool at a table in the corner and a sectional couch had been set up in front of a large flat screen TV. A tall bookshelf held a myriad of books and board games. The remainder of the room contained a Ping-Pong table and other table games.

"Thank goodness," Desi said. "This should keep them busy for a while. I wasn't looking forward to being cooped up with the kids in the cabin if this rain continues."

"No kidding." I scanned the room. "I wonder if they play movies for the kids on rainy evenings?"

Before she could answer me, Anthony tugged on his mom's arm. "Can we play with the soccer game?"

Desi knelt down to his level and put her arm around him. "What soccer game?"

He pointed to the foosball table. "That one."

She glanced at it. "Sure, honey."

The boys ran off to play, leaving Desi and I alone with the two babies.

"So, this isn't exactly what we'd planned for our dream family vacation." I made a face.

"Nope. I kind of thought we'd leave finding dead bodies at home, but it seems to have followed us out here. Soon they won't let you go anywhere."

"Desi! It's not my fault. These things just happen."

"To you more than others." She picked up Lina, who'd had woken up with her carrier in a strange place and was crying.

"Seriously though. I really thought we'd have a good time here. We've been looking forward to it for so long."

She sighed and bounced in place with Lina against her chest. "I know. I wish Tomàs was here." She glanced out the window as if he might suddenly appear.

"You'll get to talk to him soon." I checked on the boys. They hadn't yet managed to knock each other out with the foosball handles, although the handles were clanking hard against the wooden table. "I'm worried about Leah though. She and Del seemed devastated by Jed's death."

"I know. This has to be horrible for them."

"Yeah. I just wish there was something I could do for her."

Desi patted my arm. "I'm sure you'll think of something." She jutted out her chin to a point behind me. "Speaking of Leah ..."

I turned around and smiled as Leah approached us.

"Your table is ready." She glanced at the boys and grinned. "They seem to be enjoying the foosball table."

"They really are," Desi agreed. "It's nice you have such a large indoor recreation area for the kids." She stood and called out to the boys that it was time to eat.

"It's one of the first changes we made to the resort when we bought it." Leah looked around the room with pride.

"This used to be a storage area, but we knew having an indoor game area would be a big draw for potential guests."

"Well, I think it's great," Desi said.

Mikey ran past me and I caught him by his sleeve. "I'd better get going before he's halfway across the camp."

She smiled. "Have a nice dinner. Oh, and if you wouldn't mind, could you stop by my house tonight? Maybe around eight? I'd love to catch up with you."

I hesitated before answering. On one hand, it had been a while since I'd last had a real conversation with Leah and I missed hanging out with her. On the other hand, I was here with my family and I didn't want to do too much that would take me away from them. But Leah had just been through a traumatic event with Jed's murder, and judging by the interaction I'd witnessed between her and Del, she could probably use a friendly ear. Besides, the kids would already be asleep by eight.

"Sure, I'd love to too. See you later." I let Mikey pull me away and we joined Adam at the table for dinner.

7

Once the kids were asleep for the night, I managed to slip out to see Leah at her house. The rain had stopped for a bit, but the ground underneath my feet squished out water with every step. At eight o'clock, the resort was dark and I let my fears take over, quickening my pace whenever I neared any large bushes or trees that someone could hide behind. By the time I reached her house, I had to caution myself not to run up the steps and bang on the door like a girl in a campy horror movie.

I'd only seen Leah's house from a distance before, but now that I was closer, I could appreciate how carefully she maintained the house. Although the flower beds were soggy and the petunias hung limply on their stems from the weight of the recent rain, the colors were still cheery. The two-story log cabin had been recently stained and a swing hung from the roof of the small porch.

I knocked on the door and Leah answered right away.

"Jill, I'm so happy to see you. Come in." She gestured to the small living room right inside the door. "Do you want anything to drink? I have coffee, tea, or wine." She picked up a glass of wine from a round end table. "I'm having some Merlot."

It was definitely that kind of day. "I'll have a glass too. Thanks."

While she fetched my wine, I looked around the living room. A leather couch had been pushed up against one wall, facing the television, and an armchair was situated at a ninety-degree angle from the couch. An incongruously small picture hung crookedly over the fireplace. A few photos of Leah and an older couple who I presumed were her parents hung on the wall. I didn't see any pictures of Del.

Leah returned, handing me my glass. She perched on the edge of the armchair while I sat down on the couch.

"Is Del home?" I hadn't heard anyone else in the house, but I didn't want to be too noisy if he was trying to sleep or something.

She bit her lip and averted her eyes. "Del and I have separated."

"Oh, Leah. I'm so sorry to hear that." My heart hurt for my friend, but it did explain a few things I'd noticed between her and Del.

"Me too." She twisted her wedding ring around her finger. "I thought we'd be the couple that would make it."

"Have you been separated for a while?"

"For a couple of months."

I leaned forward and put my hand on hers. "I really am sorry."

"Thanks."

"So how is everything else? The resort is beautiful."

"It's going pretty good, but this wasn't how I pictured your visit." She frowned. "I wanted you to see it at its best. But now it's stormy and with Jed's death, I can't imagine seeing it at a worse time." A tear came to her eye. "I still can't believe he's gone. He was involved with some shady characters in the short time he's been in Washington, but I didn't think it was anything bad enough to get him killed. Del is just torn up."

I nodded sympathetically. "He must be so upset to lose his only family member." I sipped my wine and then set it down on the end table. I was itching to ask her more about Jed's past, but now didn't seem like a good time. Besides, it wasn't really any of my business. "With the two of you being separated it must be doubly difficult for both of you. You know, you always seemed so perfect together. I'm sorry things didn't work out."

"Yeah, well, I thought things were great too." She wiped her eyes. "And then he hit me with the bombshell that he wanted a separation. He said we'd grown apart over the years and that I'd become obsessed with this place." She peered at me through a haze of tears. "He may have been right, but the resort is important to me. We sunk everything into it. He doesn't seem to understand that."

I scooted toward her and gave her a hug. "I'm sorry, Leah. It must be difficult to manage this place. Does Del help with things around here still?"

She nodded. "Yes. We're going to continue to jointly own the resort after the divorce is finalized. Whatever is left of the resort at least." She uttered a hard laugh.

I narrowed my eyes at my friend. "What do you mean 'if anything is left'?"

Leah hung her head and then looked up at me, tears in her eyes. "I've put everything I have into the business. We were fully booked through September and I'd counted on that money. Now, my e-mail inbox is full of cancellations from people who've heard about Jed's death on the news.

Heck, a quarter of the people that were already here for this week left as soon as they found out about what happened to him."

My stomach churned. I hadn't said anything to Leah about the possibility of us leaving, and now I felt bad even considering it. She didn't deserve any of this. When we'd found a client's body at the Boathouse, it had temporarily decimated our business. I didn't want to hurt Leah by cancelling our reservation too. I crossed my fingers, hoping that Tomàs would be ok with us staying for the rest of the week.

"But it's the week before Labor Day. Maybe you can get other people to stay here instead? I'd think all the campgrounds in the area are fully booked for the weekend."

Hope crossed her face, but then left just as quickly. "We were supposed to host 'Labor Day at the Lake' here this weekend. Now, what if people don't show up?" Tears were falling freely down her cheeks now. "Jill, what if people don't come? This is our big event of the year."

I hugged her. "I'm sure it will be fine. What do you have planned?" I didn't know whether having a big event at the resort so soon after a man was murdered there would be good or bad for business. Either it would bring additional people to the resort, or everyone would stay away due to the stigma of a recent murder on the grounds.

"Um, a canoe race, some field games, and a barbecue."

"Well, that all sounds like fun. I'm sure Adam and Mikey will be excited to participate." I crossed my fingers that Tomàs wouldn't want us to leave and we'd still be there this weekend.

"It would have been, but I think it's going to fall apart. Jed was in charge of the barbecue and some of the games, and I don't have time to figure out what he'd planned."

She peered up at me. "You have experience planning events now, right? Isn't that what you do?"

I groaned inwardly. I could see where this was going. I forced a smile for my friend. "Yes, I manage events at the Boathouse now."

"Do you think you could help me with the celebration? I'd really appreciate it." She quickly added, "I can't afford to pay you, but I could comp your cabin for a few nights. Would that work?"

I sighed. I couldn't let Leah lose money. She'd always been a good friend to me and had saved my bacon several times when we'd worked together. "Of course I'll help you."

She threw her arms around me. "Oh, thank you, thank you. You have no idea how much this means to me."

I smiled. "What are friends for?"

"Yeah, but most friends wouldn't take the time to help with something like this. And don't worry, you should still have plenty of time to spend with your family. I know this is your vacation."

I patted her shoulder. "I'm sure it will all work out. Do you know what Jed had planned for the barbecue? Had he ordered the food already, or were you planning on picking food up at the grocery store in town?"

"Have you seen the size of that store?" She laughed. "No, he placed an order with the barbecue place in town about a month ago. They do catering as well as service in their own restaurant. We're expecting about two hundred people, both guests of the resort and folks from town. I can get you the information tomorrow about the catering. Does that work?"

My mind was spinning. I had an event to plan that may or may not have already been planned, and it was happening in a week.

I took a deep breath. "Sure, that will work."

A look of relief passed across her face. "That's a big stressor off my plate." She scrunched up her face. "Now if I can figure out how to get people to stop cancelling the bookings, we'd be doing great."

"Can Del help more?"

"No," she said tightly, "this event isn't something he wanted to do."

I sat back. "Del doesn't want the celebration? Isn't it a good thing for the resort? I would imagine it will be great publicity."

"Yes, but it is also costly. Last year we barely broke even. He was worried before that we wouldn't make our money back on it, and now even more so this year because of Jed's death. I keep telling him that it's an investment in our future.

"Anyway, enough with all these depressing details. How are things going with you? How is working for your in-laws at the event center?"

"It can be stressful, but all in all, it's going great. I've had a little bit of an adjustment period after being home with the kids for a few years, but I think it will work out well. Adam is in the process of setting up his practice in downtown Ericksville, so the money is nice too."

She nodded. "I know it was difficult for Del and me to go from earning high salaries in our corporate careers to buying this place. Instead of taking trips to Hawaii, now we're taking fishing trips out on the lake." She glanced out the window and looked back at me fiercely. "But I don't regret it. Sometimes I feel like I was meant to be out here. There's just something about being out in nature and getting to share it with all of the resort guests. Most of them are refugees from the city and this is a whole new experience for them." She laughed. "I know it was for me."

"So, you like it here though? No thoughts of selling and moving back to Seattle?"

"Nope. None at all for me."

I noticed she hadn't mentioned Del, but I didn't want to pry into it. The situation between them seemed precarious and I didn't want to further rock the boat.

I checked my watch. "Thanks for the glass of wine, but I'd better get back to the cabin soon. Ella still wakes up sometimes in the middle of the night and I don't think Adam will hear her." I shook my head. "That man could sleep through anything."

"Del is like that too," she said. "I used to joke that he wouldn't notice a fire alarm going off next to his head. It's probably a good thing we didn't have any kids together." Her voice had a wistful note.

I pressed my lips together and then said, "I'm sorry. This must be so hard for you. I really thought you two would make it."

"Well, I suppose there's always hope." She waved me toward the door. "You'd better get going then. Don't let me keep you."

She walked me to the door, standing on the threshold as I walked down the porch steps. After I was about twenty feet away, I turned and saw her still standing there, staring out at the lake with a vacant expression on her face. What had happened to the happy-go-lucky woman I'd known back in Seattle? She'd told me how much she loved being out here, so it must be the separation from Del and her worries about the resort that were making her so sad. I hated to see her like this and I was determined to help her in any way I could during our short stay at the resort. I owed her that much.

8

To my amazement, the sky the next morning was a beautiful shade of blue, much as it had been when we'd arrived. My spirits lifted immediately. Adam and I made a hearty breakfast of eggs, bacon, and pancakes, and we sat with Desi and the kids out on the deck overlooking the water to enjoy the food and view.

"You can almost forget how horrible yesterday was when seeing this," Desi said as she looked out over the glass-smooth lake.

A canoe slid across the water and a bird flitted down near the shore in front of our deck, breaking the peace but somehow adding to the enchantment of the scene.

I shuddered. "I don't think I'll ever forget that." My eyes slid over to the boys, who were now playing a game involving a bouncy ball and a pile of sticks. We'd managed to keep them away from the ugliness that had happened yesterday, and I intended to keep it that way.

"Tomàs should be here after lunchtime. He'd planned to leave our house around seven. At this point, even if I could call him, he'd be halfway here already." Desi took a bite of eggs and then pushed her almost empty plate away.

"Oh." I'd almost forgotten that we'd agreed to let Tomàs decide whether it was safe for us to stay at the resort. "Desi, Adam, I need to talk to you about something."

"What?" Adam said, turning to face me from his seat by the railing. "Is something wrong?"

"No, it's just that I think I want to stay at the resort for the whole week." I clinked my fork against my cup while I waited for their response.

"Ok," Adam said slowly. "What made you change your mind?"

I sighed. "Leah needs me. The resort is losing money and she has this big celebration planned for next weekend. She asked if I'd help with it."

"Can't she get someone else to do it?" Desi asked.

"No. Unfortunately, Jed was scheduled to manage most of it. Now that he's gone ..."

"Ugh." Desi swirled cold coffee around in her mug. "I can see why you'd want to stay and help your friend, but is it safe?"

"I don't know," I said honestly. "When Tomàs gets here, let's talk. Maybe you and the kids can leave and I'll come home later."

"I don't know if I'm ok with that." Adam leaned against the railing and eyed me.

I picked up my plate and stacked it with the other dirty plates on the table. I grabbed the whole pile and walked toward the kitchen with them.

"Jill! Did you hear me?" Adam called.

I poked my head around the door. "Yes. Just give me a chance to think about it, ok?"

"Ok."

I stood at the sink and washed the dishes, gazing out the window as the familiar sensations of hot sudsy water lulled me into a contemplative state. I wanted to help my friend, but I didn't want to put myself or my family in danger. What was the right answer here?

I returned to the porch. "I promised Leah I'd help her. Let's see what Tomàs says when he gets here, ok?"

They nodded.

"But for now, I need to find out what Jed had planned for the Labor Day at the Lake celebration. Adam, can you take care of the kids for an hour? Maybe we can go for a hike afterwards?"

"Sure." He looked like he wanted to say more, but he clamped his mouth shut.

I kissed Mikey and Ella on their heads and left for the resort store, hoping to find Leah there. On the way, I passed a grouping of Adirondack chairs on the lawn, overlooking the lake, and couldn't help but wonder if this was where the man had crashed through a broken chair. I paused for a moment. If there was someone vandalizing the resort, could they have been responsible for Jed's death? I shuddered. That wasn't something I wanted to dwell on.

At the store, Leah was helping a customer. I waited my turn and then she grabbed something from underneath the counter and carried it out to me. It was a normal-sized spiral-bound notebook with several sheets of printer paper sticking out of the edges.

"Here's the information about the food Jed ordered." She handed me the notebook.

I flipped through it. In neat handwriting, someone had noted every detail of the food order, down to the number of ketchup bottles they were requesting.

"He was thorough."

"Yes," Leah said, "he may not have been my favorite person in the world, but he was good at planning."

I nodded. I assumed she was referring to what I'd over-heard her saying to Del about his lack of work ethic for chores around the resort.

"I can see that." I looked up from the papers. "Do you have his ideas for the games and everything else? Are there ribbons or prizes for the winners of the games?"

She frowned. "Jed should have ordered ribbons and medals for the winners from the general store in Pemberton, but I don't know if they've been picked up yet. He was taking care of all of that."

I could tell my questions were stressing her out. "No problem, I'll figure it out. Do you think he may have left some notes somewhere?"

She contemplated that. "Maybe at his house? You could try there. I think he has a desk there."

"Where is that?" Leah's house was the only one I'd seen on the property.

She walked out the door and pointed to a big red barn in the far corner of the resort.

"He lives there?" I must have looked aghast, because she laughed.

"No, Jed and Del share a mobile home on the other side of the barn. Del might not be home right now to show you around, but they always keep it unlocked. You can look around in there, he won't mind."

I nodded. "I'll take a look." I squeezed her arm. "This will all work out, stop worrying." I smiled. "You don't want to scare away any new guests, do you?"

She managed a weak smile. "No. Thank you, Jill."

"I promised Adam I'd go on a hike with him later today,

but I'll try to come by your house tonight and we can talk about this more."

"Sounds good."

I left, and Leah retreated to the back room of the office. I eyed our cabin and then the giant storage barn. I'd told Adam I'd be back in an hour, so I still had about forty-five minutes left. That should be plenty of time to check Jed's house to see if he'd left anything behind about the games for the weekend's celebration.

In front of the mobile home was an older model Ford truck, but not the red pickup truck that Del had been driving yesterday. I knocked on the metal door to the mobile home but received no response. When I tried the doorknob, it turned easily under my hand. Leah had been right—Del hadn't bothered to lock the door.

Inside the mobile home, the curtains were all shut. I blinked, allowing my eyes to adjust to the dark as I searched for the light switch. I felt blindly along the wall, finally locating it about a foot inside the door. I flipped it on, allowing a weak light to bathe the small living room. An orange and brown couch sat in front of an old box TV. The floor was littered with used Kleenexes and a half-empty bottle of whiskey sat on the glass-topped coffee table. If I had to guess, I'd say Del had been mourning his cousin last night.

Although Leah had told me that entering Del's home was ok, I felt as though I was intruding and I wanted to get in and out of there quickly. I pushed on the first door in the short hallway. The room was packed with sports paraphernalia and other belongings, including a beer stein bearing Del's name.

I continued on down the hallway to what I assumed had been Jed's room. The door was closed, but like the front door, the handle turned easily in my hand. I had a weird sense opening the door. The only time I'd ever seen Jed was when I discovered his body next to the campfire pit. Now I was entering his private domain. I took a deep breath and entered the room. The drapes were open in this room and the sun shone in brightly. It was sparsely furnished, with a double bed, battered wood dresser, and a small desk in the corner. Three rows of baseball hats decorated the wall behind the bed—Jed had been a collector.

I crossed the room to the desk. If I was going to find anything out about Jed's plans for the weekend celebration, they'd most likely be there. The top of the desk was bare. I opened the center drawer, but it held only pens and pencils. The top drawer on the side bore more fruit.

I pulled out a pad of lined paper. In the same neat script as the food order, Jed had written a list of games that he'd intended to offer that weekend. But where would he have put the ribbons—if any? I rummaged around in the other drawer and came up with nothing.

I put the notebook on the perfectly made bed and opened his closet but didn't see any prizes. A few pairs of shoes were lined up in a row against the back, but otherwise, the carpeted floor was empty.

Except, what was that sticking out of the far corner? Everything else in his room had been so orderly, so why was there a bag lying haphazardly on the floor? It didn't look like it was big enough to hold prize ribbons and medals, but I figured I'd check it out anyway.

I picked it up, admiring the blue velvet, and flipped it over to see the other side. It was as blank as the front. This looked like a bag you'd get for jewelry. Leah hadn't mentioned Jed having a girlfriend, but she may not have been privy to everything in his life. I held it up in the air, but it flopped in my hands—empty. I tossed it back on the closet floor and turned back around to scan the rest of the room. Other than the baseball caps, this room was so devoid of personality that I'd almost hoped that there would be more to his life than Leah had alluded to.

I grabbed the notebook off the bed, smoothing the coverlet afterwards. I stepped out of the room and softly closed the door behind me.

Before I could reach the front door, I heard it squeak open and someone enter. Del glanced up at the light and then noticed me in the hallway. He raised an eyebrow.

"Jill? What are you doing here?"

"Sorry, I didn't mean to intrude. Leah asked me to manage the event portion of the Labor Day at the Lake celebration, but I didn't have any idea of what Jed had been working on. She said I could come in here to look for the winner's ribbons and get his notes from his room." I held up the notebook.

"Ah. No problem." He stepped forward. "Do you want anything to drink?" His face reddened as if he had just noticed the mess in his living room. He scooped up most of the wadded-up Kleenexes and the whiskey bottle and carried them in to the kitchen. "Sorry for the mess. I was up early this morning cleaning up debris from the storm."

"Oh, no problem. Were there any trees down in the resort?"

He shook his head. "No. We routinely check for dead or diseased trees, so we don't usually have a problem with them falling down in storms. The branches, on the other hand, we can't really control. At least I didn't have to worry about watering this morning." He guffawed.

"No kidding. I think we got enough rain for weeks. You

must have been frustrated when it rained so soon after you watered on Monday morning."

Del's face fell. "I'm sure I would have been, but I didn't water that morning like usual. I'd had a late night, and Jed offered to do the watering and other morning chores for me so I could sleep. I wonder if he'd be alive today if I'd been out there instead of him. Maybe it was a case of him being in the wrong place at the wrong time. The medical examiner said he died around 4 a.m., so it must have happened right after he started watering."

"Maybe. I'm so sorry for your loss, Del. Leah told me that he was your only remaining family."

"Yes, he was." His voice quivered. "His parents died when we were young and my parents raised him. When they died a few years ago we drifted apart, but because of our upbringing, we've always had a tight bond."

"Do the police have any idea of who killed him?"

He shook his head. "I don't think so. They interviewed me for a long time yesterday down at the police station. They asked me about some of his acquaintances here, but he didn't associate with many people other than me. Maybe a few guys down at Rex's Place that I don't know."

I nodded. Were the guys down at Rex's the "shady characters" Leah had mentioned? If so, could they have been responsible for Jed's death?

"Well, I'm really sorry for your loss. If there's anything I can do while I'm here, please let me know." I jutted my thumb at the door. "I told my husband I'd be back about fifteen minutes ago, so I'd better get going."

"Oh." He sounded sad that I was leaving. "I'll see you around."

9

*W*hen I returned to our cabin, a familiar car was parked in front of Desi's cabin—Tomàs had arrived. His voice rang out from the deck and I walked toward it with trepidation. I'd promised Leah to help her with the celebration, but I wasn't sure Tomàs would think that was a good idea. I respected his opinion as a seasoned police officer, but I'd made a commitment to my friend to stay and I'd miss Adam and the kids if they left early. Well, that is if Adam was ok with me staying. He seemed genuinely worried about me, and although I wanted to stay, I didn't want to do so if he had reservations.

The adults were sitting in Adirondack chairs on the deck, right where I'd left them. From the racket coming from inside the cabin, I guessed that Mikey and Anthony were playing something involving cars with revving engines.

Desi heard my approach and greeted me. "Hey, we were just about to send out a search party."

"Sorry, I ended up talking to Del and it took me longer than I'd expected. But I got Jed's notes on the plans for the celebration. Hey, Tomàs."

He smiled at me.

"Jill," Adam said, patting the empty chair next to him. "I'm glad you're back. We've been telling Tomàs about everything that's been going on here."

"And?" I made my way over to the empty chair and peered at Tomàs. He didn't look happy.

"I wish Desi had been able to call me earlier." He looked around. "I'd like to talk with local law enforcement about the case, before we make any decisions." He ran his fingers through his short brown hair. "I swear, trouble seems to follow you and Desi everywhere."

His wife lightly slugged his arm in response. "It does not."

"You know it does. In the short amount of time you've been here, there's been a robbery at the jewelry store and a murder at the resort." He feigned a stern look at her. "But in all seriousness, I want to go into town to talk to someone at the police department about this." He leaned forward. "Maybe they've already figured this out and we're worrying for nothing."

Adam cleared his throat. "Since the weather has cleared up and we may not be staying much longer, I thought I'd take Mikey out on the trail behind the resort. Would it be ok if I took Anthony too?"

Tomàs glanced at his son, weighing his decision. He looked at Desi, who nodded. "I think that would be fine."

"I'd like to go with you to town if there's room," I said, idly running my fingers over the smooth wood on the chair arms. As with everything else I'd seen at the resort, they'd been exquisitely maintained. "I need to check on the ribbons for the Labor Day event."

Tomàs raised his eyebrow. "Are you working on an event

here? I thought you two were excited to get away from all that."

Desi came over to me and wrapped an arm around my shoulder. "We were, but Jill's friend Leah, the owner of the resort, asked her to help. I think it's great that she's willing to help out."

I looked at her gratefully. "Thanks, Desi." I turned to Adam. "I promise helping out with this event won't take up too much of my time."

He smiled at me. "It's ok, honey—I would actually be more surprised if you didn't help out a friend in need—but I do want to make sure it's safe for you to stay." He walked over to the boys and knelt down beside them, talking to them in a low voice.

Their eyes lit up and they ran to the door before Adam could even straighten up to a full standing position. He laughed and joined the boys at the door. They left, with Adam running after them, shouting for them to wait for him. I could already tell that this was going to be a *fun* hike for him.

"Well, I guess they won't miss us," Desi said.

I laughed. "Let's get going before Adam changes his mind about taking both of them. I'd like to get to the store before lunchtime."

Tomàs jingled his keys. "I'm ready whenever you two are."

Desi, Tomàs, the babies, and I piled into Desi's minivan for the trip into town. I sat in the back seat with the two girls in their car seats, while Desi sat in the front seat next to Tomàs.

They were talking about some maintenance issue at their house, so I tuned them out and stared out the window as we passed through dense forests. Soon, the trees cleared out a little and we began to see signs of civilization on the outskirts of Pemberton.

I leaned forward. "Tomàs, can you drop me off at the general store? Leah told me Jed ordered the winners' ribbons from them."

He glanced at me through the rearview mirror. "Sure, I can do that. Do you want me to pick you up at a certain time?"

"No, I'll give you a call. Pemberton gets fairly decent cell service. Does that work for you?"

Desi turned around. "We were planning on grabbing lunch. Did you want to join us?"

I figured they had a lot to talk about and could use some privacy. I'd made it clear that I didn't want to leave the resort and I didn't want that to influence their decision about whether to stay or not. Also, this seemed like the perfect time to satisfy my curiosity about the velvet bag I'd found in Jed's closet. After finding out from Leah that Jed had been involved with some shady characters, part of me wondered if he'd been the one who'd robbed the jewelry store. It was probably a crazy theory, but I hoped to find out if the jewelry store in town even used the same type of bag.

I shook my head. "No, I'll find something. I forgot to bring a book to read, so I'm going to check out the bookstore too." I deliberately didn't tell them I planned to visit the jewelry store as that was bound to bring up some questions.

She shrugged. "Ok, but let me know if you change your mind."

Tomàs pulled into a spot in the general store's parking

lot and popped the liftgate. I unbuckled myself and Ella and met him at the back of the minivan where he set up my folding stroller.

"Thanks." I strapped Ella securely into her seat. "I'm glad I remembered to bring this thing with us on the trip. I felt like I was bringing everything but the kitchen sink, and then I almost forgot this—one of the most important things."

He nodded. "Good thing you did. Babies get heavy after a while and it's such a nice day for a stroll."

Tomàs walked toward the driver's side and glanced at me as I wheeled Ella a few feet away. He pushed on the liftgate and it closed. He stuck his hands in his pants pockets and shifted on his feet.

"You sure you don't want to join us for lunch?"

I smiled at him. "I'm sure. Ella and I may do a picnic in the park." Across the street, a tree-lined park with bright green grass beckoned for us to come and play in it.

He held up a finger. "In that case, wait." He opened the rear door again and rummaged around in there, then handed me a heavy plaid blanket. "You can use this for your picnic."

"Thanks." I stuck it in the basket under the stroller. "This will come in handy."

He shut the door again. "Give us a call when you're ready to be picked up."

"I will." I swiveled the stroller around and headed into the general store.

Outside the automatic sliding glass doors of the store, hanging baskets filled with colorful blue, purple, and orange flowers swung in the light breeze, filling the air with an intoxicating scent. Other customers ambled across the parking lot and into the store, sending a blast of air-conditioning in our direction. I followed them in, surprised to see that it was bigger than it had looked from the outside.

I approached the customer service desk and was greeted warmly by the clerk.

"Can I help you with anything, miss?" the elderly man asked while smiling at Ella.

"Jed from the Thunder Lake Resort had ordered some ribbons. Do you know if they've been picked up yet?"

"Ah yes. I know what you're talking about. They came in a few days ago, but no one showed up to pick them up." He held up a finger. "Wait one moment and I'll go get those for you."

I leaned against the counter, taking in all the things behind the counter, which ranged from guns to tobacco products to lottery tickets.

"Here we are," he said upon return. He handed me a large package. "They should all be there."

I quickly checked the contents. There were ribbons with first, second, and third place on them, as well as participant awards. For the boat race, Jed had ordered a gold medal for the winner. All were imprinted with the name of the resort and the year.

"Looks good."

"Say, I was sorry to hear about Jed. Please give my condolences to Del and Leah."

"I will. Did you know Jed well?"

"No, he came in here a couple of times, but I saw him down at Rex's Place quite often when I'd go in for a beer after work. As far as I know, that's really the only place he ever went in town when not on work business. He wasn't real friendly with folks in town."

Hmm ... Rex's Place. I was pretty sure that was the bar Del had mentioned too. I smiled at the clerk and stuck the package in the bottom of Ella's stroller. "Thank you for this. I'd better go and feed the little one, but I hope you have a nice day!"

He waved and said, "You too."

I wheeled her out of the store and then paused in the shade from the roof overhang. What were we going to do next? I'd told Tomàs he didn't need to pick me up for a while, and I was starting to get hungry. First though, I wanted to see if the velvet bag I'd found in Jed's closet had come from the jewelry store.

I stopped outside of Junell Jewelry, but the hand-printed sign on the door announced that they wouldn't be open for a few more days due to remodeling. I tried to peer in the window but didn't see much construction going on in the retail area of the store. Was it closed due to the robbery earlier in the week?

I turned to Ella. "What next, baby girl?"

She smiled at me and babbled something incoherent.

"Food? Yes, I think you're right."

She looked at me like I was crazy, which could be an accurate perception as I was talking to a nine-month-old baby like she could understand me. There weren't many food options in town but the local café had a sign on their window stating that they sold picnic lunches. Perfect.

I selected a picnic lunch package from them, and we took our lunch over to the park to eat. I'd forgotten to bring the sunscreen with us. I didn't want to risk looking like a lobster for the rest of the week, so I hoped I'd be able to score a spot in the shade. Luckily, I found somewhere to place the blanket under the shade from a tall tree.

My mouth watered as I unwrapped the Havarti and

turkey on focaccia bread sandwich that the café had prepared for me. Ella eyed me with disdain, opening and closing her mouth in a sucking motion. I laughed and peeled the lid off of the container of tapioca pudding they'd included, spooning some into her mouth. She greedily ate it then sucked down the bottle I'd brought for her in a small freezer bag.

We watched as two squirrels chased each other across the grass then climbed the tree across from us in a zig-zag pattern. Ella giggled and pointed. While I ate the sandwich, she leaned forward to pluck pieces of grass from the ground, watching in wonder as they drifted through her fingers as they fell to the ground. When were finished, I sat back against the tree and contemplated what was next for our visit to town. I needed to make a quick stop in the barbecue place to check on the arrangements for the Labor Day celebration, but I also hoped to find out a little more about Jed. There had to be some reason he'd been killed, and I refused to believe that there was a murderer on the loose, randomly killing innocent people. That seemed a little too far-fetched.

The clerk in the general store had mentioned Rex's Place. Somebody there might know more about Jed. I packed up our belongings and put Ella back in the stroller. How was I going to find the bar though? I didn't remember seeing it on the main drag through town. I'd forgotten to charge my cell phone since I couldn't use it back at the resort anyway, so I didn't want use up all of the battery staring at a map.

A man walked in front of us, carrying a paper sack that smelled like hamburgers.

"Excuse me," I said, flagging him down.

"Oh, hi." The man smiled at me and Ella. "Sorry, didn't see you there."

"I was wondering if you could tell me where Rex's was."

He cocked his head to the side, as if wondering why I'd want to go there. Then he pointed to the end of the block.

"It's down there, about a block off Main Street."

"Thank you." I turned in the opposite direction to walk toward the bar. I hoped that it was more of a pub than a bar that didn't serve food. In Washington State, minors weren't allowed in bars and I didn't think I'd be able to convince anyone that Ella was over twenty-one.

When I reached Rex's, my hopes were dashed. The brick building had a big sign on the door proclaiming NO MINORS ALLOWED. Although I'd hoped we'd be allowed in, I couldn't help but grin at the sign, remembering a story my mother told me about how when she was young, she'd seen a similar sign and wondered what they'd had against miners.

I had turned to leave, when a man walked out, carrying a bucket of water and a sponge. He set it down in front of the glass windows and swiped at some smudges in the glass.

"Hey, do you work here?" I asked.

"No, I just really like to go around wiping down all the windows in town." He smiled at me to let me know he was joking. "I'm the general manager here. Can I help you with something?"

"I'm friends with Del and Leah over at the Thunder Lake Resort. I was hoping you might know something about Del's cousin Jed, who died recently." I hoped he wouldn't ask why I wanted to know.

"Well, you won't find out much here. I don't think many people knew Jed well, although he was in here often. He didn't have many friends as he owed several people money. I'd venture a guess that one of them killed him when they found out he planned to skip town." He dipped the sponge in the water and then squeezed out the excess water.

So, Jed owed people money. That confirmed my impression from Leah that he wasn't always an upstanding citizen.

"Wait, he was planning to leave town?"

The man shrugged. "He was bragging to everyone that he'd come into some money, and he and Del were going to open a business somewhere—I'm not sure where."

"Did he say where the money came from?" Was this the answer to my question? Had Jed stolen the diamonds? Was that why he was killed? The more I thought about it, the crazier the idea seemed.

He tilted his head to the side. "As far as I know, he never said. Why do you want to know anyway?"

"Any information is good to have." I smiled brightly at him. "I'd better get my baby out of the heat though. Thank you so much for your help."

He narrowed his eyes at me but just nodded.

It was almost two o'clock and I was ready to head back to the resort. I stopped in at the barbecue restaurant and checked on the catering order for the Labor Day celebration. Everything was good to go with them, so Ella and I walked back to the park, stopping in the shade. I plucked my phone out of my purse to call Tomàs to pick us up but decided to try Danielle again to see if she had gotten my message about preschool registration.

The phone rang and rang, then went to voice mail. I'd have to try again another day. Every day that passed made me more nervous that I'd be out of luck getting Mikey registered. But there was nothing more I could do about it. While I had cell service, I should probably call Beth to check on everything at home, but I didn't want to bother her at work during the day. With me and Desi gone, she had enough to do without me bugging her.

I rang Tomàs, and he and Desi came to pick us up. After I snapped Ella's carrier into the base, I hopped into the back of their minivan.

"Did you find anything out from the local police?" I held my breath, waiting for his response.

Tomàs regarded me in the rearview mirror. "They said that Jed had some mishaps in his past and it wasn't likely we were in any danger. After reviewing the facts, I'm inclined to agree."

"So, we can stay?" I'd hoped, but I hadn't really expected Tomàs to be ok with letting us stay.

Desi turned around in the passenger seat and grinned at me. "Yup."

I exhaled. Thank goodness. I hadn't wanted to go against what the rest of my family chose to do, but I didn't want to let Leah down either. Now though, I was curious. What were the facts about Jed's murder that Tomàs had reviewed? I considered asking him, but didn't want to do anything that would make him suspicious that I was sleuthing again.

With a wide smile on my face, I said, "Let's try to forget this happened, ok? I want us to have fun for the rest of our trip. Agreed?"

To satisfy my own curiosity, I still intended to try to figure out why Jed had the velvet bag in his closet, but I wasn't going to launch a full-on investigation into his death. The police could handle that, and finding a murderer wasn't why we were at the lake.

"Agreed," Desi and Tomàs said.

He hit a button on the dashboard and classical music filled the car. In the front seat they chatted between themselves and I leaned back against my seat, watching the trees blur together as we whizzed by. Between the monotonous scenery and the whir of the air-conditioning, I almost fell asleep. By the time we returned to the resort, my brain had relaxed and I felt full and content, ready to start our fun family vacation.

10

*a*fter we'd cleared away the dinner dishes, Adam and Mikey sat down on the floor to play a game of Hungry Hungry Hippos that we'd checked out from the office. I sat down next to them.

"I need to give your mom a call to find out how things are going back at our house and at the Boathouse. Are you good here?" I asked.

Adam glanced at Ella, who was rolling around on a blanket on the thick rag rug.

"We're good." He threw a couple of marbles in the center of the hippo pit. "Hey, can you make sure that they've watered my rose garden?"

I rolled my eyes. Ever since he'd left his corporate job, he'd become obsessed with our yard. I half expected to find him out there someday, measuring the length of the grass with a ruler. Oh well, at least he was home with us more now.

I smiled. "I'll ask. Anything else?"

"Nope." He turned back to their game. "Hey Mikey, you're cheating! You only get to play one hippo."

Mikey giggled and smashed his hands down on two of the four hippos. "I'm going to beat you, Daddy!"

The game was heating up so I left before a stray marble could hit me on the head and walked over to the pay phone, which was located outside, behind the office. Leah and Del had placed a bench next to the phone booth in case there was a line, but right now it was empty. In the morning, this was most likely in full sun, but at this time of day, the roof of the office shaded the whole area.

I inserted my credit card. This was one of the first pay phones I'd seen in a long time, but it made sense out here where there wasn't cell service. I had Beth's number programmed into my phone, but I didn't know her number offhand, so I had to search for it in my phone's address book. Thank goodness for technology. Even without cell reception, I kept my phone with me at all times—unlike the address book I used to have that never left my house. I scrolled through the names and punched her digits into the pay phone.

"Hello?" she asked, sounding puzzled.

"Hey," I said. "It's me, Jill."

"Jill? Where are you calling from?"

"A pay phone at the resort. I wanted to check in with you about how everything is going with our house and at work."

She laughed. "Honey, you're supposed to be enjoying your vacation, not worrying about everything back here. Everything's fine—well, except for that lady with the Halloween party we scheduled last spring. She is driving me nuts."

I grimaced. "Angela is almost worse than a nervous bride."

"Almost?" Beth chuckled again. "She makes brides look like angels."

"What does she want now?" I'd called Angela to check in with her before we left for Eastern Washington, but she hadn't called back.

"Oh, everything. She wants to confirm all the details—the fog machine, the lighting, parking—just everything."

"Oh well, hosting the Ericksville Haunted House this year could be good for business. It's a fall booking and it will be a good promo for the Boathouse." I fanned the air in front of me. Even though the phone booth was in the shade, the semi-enclosed space was heating up.

"I guess. Maybe I'm getting too old for this. I can't deal with the crazies as well as I used to." She sighed into the phone.

"You're not too old," I said automatically. However, Beth had gone through heart surgery about a month earlier, and although everything seemed fine with her, I didn't want to be stressing her too much. "Are you ok with everything there?"

"Of course I am," she said in a cheerier voice. "Lincoln and I can run this place with our hands tied behind our backs."

"I feel bad about leaving you." I wrapped the coiled phone line around my fingers, watching the metal twist into a circle. I missed doing that with cell phones.

"Don't even worry about it. I know you and Desi have been looking forward to this vacation for a long time. How's it going out there anyway? I haven't heard anything from her."

"Uh ..." I wasn't sure how much to tell her. "Things here have been fine. I'm actually going to be helping my friend Leah out with their Labor Day celebration. It sounds like it will be a lot of fun." I toed the dirt next to the concrete pad and took a deep breath. I might as well tell her now as she was bound to find out from someone. "We had some excitement the first morning though. I kind of found another body."

She was quiet for a moment. "Another one? It was a natural death though, right?"

"Uh ..."

"Jill! What's going on there?" Her voice held a note of panic. "Are you all ok?"

"The man who died was the cousin of my friend Leah's husband. Apparently he had made some enemies in the past."

"Are you safe there? What does Tomàs think?"

"He talked to the local law enforcement and they said not to worry." I chose not to tell her about the vandalism at the resort.

"Ok then." She sounded doubtful. "How is everything else? Have Mikey and Anthony gone fishing? They were both so excited about it. They even got Lincoln to show them how to put a worm on a hook."

"Eww. I think they're using some other kind of bait." Adam had said something about marshmallows. "I think Tomàs and Adam plan to take them out later in the week."

"Good. And the girls?"

"Eh, Ella seems to like it. It will be more fun going places with her next year when she's walking." I tried to turn the subject away from the resort. "How's Fluffy?" We'd left our cat at home, but Beth and Lincoln were feeding her every day.

"Oh yeah. A funny story. She may be a little pudgier than when you left."

"What happened?"

"Lincoln didn't get the top of the food container latched and she knocked it over. I think she had a heyday with the unlimited food before we found it tipped over last night."

I sighed. Fluffy loved her food and could easily eat four times the amount that was advisable.

"Just keep an eye on her in case she gets sick."

"We will. But, surprisingly, she came running to us when we opened the door this morning and wanted more food."

I laughed. "She can never get enough. Thank you again for taking care of everything while we're gone. Oh, and Adam wants to make sure you've been watering his roses."

She laughed. "Of course. Tell him not to worry about the garden. The roses are blooming and gorgeous. In fact, I cut one to display in a vase on my kitchen table. It's making my house smell heavenly." Her tone sobered. "I'm glad you were able to go as a family, although it does concern me that there was a murder at the campground."

I wound the cord tighter around my fingers. "Tomàs isn't worried, so I'm sure everything is fine."

"If you say so." She coughed. "I'd better go, I've developed a summer cold and it's making me a little hoarse. I probably shouldn't be talking this much if I want to have any voice left by tomorrow."

I hated that she was taking so much on while she was sick. "Are you sure you don't want us to come back?"

"No. It's just a little cough. Nothing to worry about. I'm sure I'll be fine by tomorrow."

"Ok." I stared at the pay phone. I hoped she was telling me the truth. "But let us know if you need us to come back early."

"I will," she said. "Now, go have fun. Enjoy the sun."

"Bye, Beth."

"Goodbye. Tell the others that I love them, and I hope they're having fun."

"Ok." I set the phone in the cradle and leaned against the frame of the pay phone enclosure. Although I wanted to help Leah at the resort and I didn't want to admit this to Tomàs, I had some reservations about staying there. Finding a body the first day we were there hadn't exactly set the tone for a relaxing vacation. And now, Beth was sick. But, for the sake of my family and my friend, I needed to make the best of it. I took a deep breath. *Fake it until you make it, Jill.*

I walked away from the phone booth, heading toward the lake. The sky was a beautiful shade of blue, and other than the tree branches and other debris on the ground, which Del and the rest of the resort staff was slowly clearing away, you'd never guess it had been storming for the last few days.

That night, I left the kids asleep in the cabin and Adam reading a book on his tablet and went to Leah's house to check in with her about the Labor Day celebration. It was in less than a week, and I wasn't sure everything had been squared away.

"Hey Jill, come in." She held the door open for me. "I was just heating some water for tea. Do you want some?"

"I'd love a cup of something herbal. If I drink caffeine at this time of night, I'll never get to sleep." I followed her into the kitchen where she had a teapot on the stove, steam shooting out the top of it.

"Me neither. I was going to have peppermint. Does that work for you? I think I have chamomile somewhere too." She rummaged around in the pantry then emerged with both boxes of tea in hand.

"Peppermint sounds great."

She plopped teabags into two cups and poured the hot water over them, then handed one to me. We settled down on the couch in the living room and I inhaled the sweet minty aroma.

"So how are things going with the event preparation?" Leah peered at me over the top of her cup.

"It seems like everything's pretty much under control. I checked on the catering and the barbecue restaurant in town is on top of everything." I leaned forward. I wondered how everything was going for Leah. She had seemed upset the last time I talked with her, and I wanted to find out if there was anything else I could do to help her. "How's everything with you?"

"Oh great, great. I'm sure the town is going to love the celebration. We've done it for the last couple of years, and it's been great publicity for the resort."

"That must help to bring in new customers. And I bet the resort guests love it too."

She took a huge gulp of tea, which must have burned her tongue. "Actually, I don't want to lie to you." She looked me directly in the eyes. "Things haven't been going so well at the resort. With the wildfires last year, we lost a lot of business and we haven't been able to recoup those losses yet. Del doesn't think we'll get many people to come this year. I think he's wrong though. Having this event go smoothly could mean the difference between keeping the resort and selling it."

"Oh, Leah, I'm sorry. That's scary. I know how much this place means to you." I sat back, stunned by how much my friend was dealing with right then. Between financial difficulties at the resort, the vandalism, and separating from her husband, it was a wonder that she hadn't given up and moved back to Seattle. "Have there been many more cancel-lations?"

She bit her lip and looked at the window that faced the lake. The sun had set, leaving only a trace of light in the sky. "Once the phone lines came back up, we had a few more cancellations. I've only had one new person make a reserva-tion for this week. We didn't need this on top of everything else."

Was "everything else" the vandalism at the resort?

"Leah." I stopped. It felt odd to tell her that I'd been eavesdropping on her and Del the evening we arrived, but I wanted to be honest with her. "The night before Jed was killed I heard you and Del arguing about the vandalism at the resort."

She looked at me in confusion. "I didn't see anybody else around."

I shifted in my seat. "Your voices carried. The windows in our cabin were open and I could hear everything you were saying."

"Oh." She wrapped her hands around her tea cup.

"Do you know who might be vandalizing the resort?"

She shook her head. "No. We've got a neighbor who isn't fond of us because of an easement dispute, but other than that, maybe someone who works here? Most of the issues have happened at night." She peered anxiously at me. "Please don't tell anyone else about this. I'd hate for the guests to find out."

"Don't worry, I don't plan on telling anyone." I reached my hand out to her. "I'm only telling you that I know about the vandalism because I want you to know that you can count on me. While I'm here, and even back in Seattle. I don't know how much help I can be from so far away, but if there's anything I can do for you, I will. I still consider you a good friend."

Her voice trembled. "Thank you. I don't have very many friends left from my former life. All I really had here was Del, and now I don't even have him." Her eyes shimmered with unshed tears.

"I'm so sorry, Leah. This must be really rough on you, with your separation from Del and everything. You didn't need all of this on top of it."

Tears dripped down her face and she brushed them away with the back of her hand. "When we bought this place, I knew it would be tough going for a while. But Del and I were so committed to making it work, and we knew we could get through anything together." She uttered a harsh laugh. "I can't believe how wrong I was about that."

I set my teacup down on the end table and gave her a hug. She lifted one arm to feebly return the embrace.

"Why do you think he wanted the separation?" I asked.

Leah shook her head. "I don't know. I guess our lives just went in different directions. I wanted to continue to make the resort a success, and Del ... I just don't know what he wants anymore." She rubbed her hand over the soft microfiber cushion on her chair. "Now with all the vandalism of the resort and Jed's murder making staying here less desirable for Del, I feel like any chance of us getting back together is getting further and further away."

"Do you think you could maybe talk to him about it? It sounds like he pulled away from you, without really telling you why."

She shrugged. "I can guess why. He thinks that the resort has taken over everything in my life." She hugged her knees to her chest and leaned her chin on them. "He's probably right, but we have everything invested in this place. If we don't make it a success, we'll have nothing."

"Look, I don't want to insert myself into your relationship, but as someone who's recently had some issues in their own marriage, I highly advise communicating more."

She looked at me teary-eyed. "You and Adam had problems?"

I nodded. "With him traveling so much, and me having most of the responsibilities for our kids, we grew apart a little. I didn't know where things were going with us, but after we talked about it a lot, he realized that he wanted to spend more time at home, so he quit his corporate job. We've had some things to work through, but we've come out the other side stronger than we ever were."

"I never knew." She gazed at me in wonder.

I laughed. "It wasn't something we publicized much. In all truthfulness, it wasn't even something we realized until it got to the point where we were almost strangers in the same house. That's why I'm saying even a little communication can go a long way. I wish we'd figured that out sooner."

She brightened a little. "Thanks. I'm not sure how things will turn out with Del or with the resort, but I appreciate the pep talk."

"No problem." I checked my watch. "I better get back. Adam and Tomàs are planning on going fishing at the crack of dawn tomorrow morning, and Desi and I were going to get up early to see them off."

"Of course, I'm sorry I kept you so late." She walked with me to the door. "I'll see you tomorrow."

She shut the door gently behind me, and I returned to our cabin where my husband was waiting for me in the living area with a glass of wine. I smiled at him, glad that we'd been

able to work on our own marriage and continue to communi-
cate about everything that was important to us. Things still
weren't perfect between us, but then again, I didn't think any
relationship was ever perfect. Every day, I was reminded more
and more of how lucky I was to have such a loving family.

11

A knock sounded on our cabin's door early the next morning. I sat up with a start and patted the other side of the bed. Empty. Where was Adam? The morning fuzzies cleared from my head and I remembered. Adam and Tomàs were going fishing. Desi and I had made plans to relax on the deck and enjoy the peace and quiet together before the kids woke up. I hurriedly threw a sweatshirt on over the yoga pants and tank top that I'd slept in and brushed my hair back.

I opened the door to the main room of the cabin and almost ran into Tomàs. He held a sleeping Anthony in his arms.

"Where should I put him?" Tomàs whispered.

I pointed at the other bedroom. "Put him in bed with Mikey."

He nodded and pushed open the door, returning in a minute with empty hands. He exited the cabin as Adam entered carrying a tackle box.

The aroma of freshly brewed coffee filled the air and I made my way over to the coffee pot on autopilot. Desi laughed and handed me a tall mug to fill. There was only a little over a cup left in the glass carafe. I wanted that caffeine, but I didn't want to be piggy.

I motioned to our husbands. "Did they get some coffee already?"

"I filled two thermoses up and I've got mine." Desi grinned at me. "Go for it."

I breathed a sigh of relief and poured the remaining coffee in my cup, then set the machine up to brew another pot. Tomàs came back in wearing a fisherman's life vest and holding another.

"Ready?" He held the vest up to Adam.

Adam nodded. "I think I have everything."

"Ok, let's go. I hear the fish are really biting at this time of day." The men left the cabin, the screen door banging closed behind them.

Desi grimaced at the sound and shot a glance at the smaller bedroom's closed door. "I'm surprised the kids didn't wake up with all that racket."

I tiptoed over to the bedroom door, and peeked in. The boys were sleeping soundly in the twin bed, sharing a single pillow. In the same room, Ella was sprawled out in her Pack 'n Play, moving slightly in her sleep as she dreamed.

I shut the door softly and retreated to the deck, where Desi sat drinking her coffee. "They're all sawing logs."

She laughed. "Yeah, sometimes Anthony can sleep through anything." She leaned over and adjusted the blanket across Lina, who was sleeping peacefully in her rocker next to the table.

The air was cool and quiet, reminding me of the first morning after our arrival when I woke up early and found Jed's body by the campfire. I shuddered. Hopefully this day would turn out better than that one had.

"This is nice." Desi sighed and leaned back in her chair, gazing out at the lake through the thicket of trees in front of our cabin.

"It is." This is what I had imagined when Desi and I had planned this vacation originally. An opportunity for us to spend time with family away from all of the commotion of everyday life.

The peaceful feeling vanished when Adam and Tomàs trudged up to the cabin, still carrying their fishing poles and tackle boxes. They stomped onto the deck and set their fishing equipment down, returning to the seats they'd vacated only twenty minutes before. Desi and I exchanged confused glances.

"Why are you back so soon?" Desi asked Tomàs.

He frowned. "Some idiot cut the mooring lines on all of the boats that were tied up at the dock."

"Every single boat is adrift on the lake," Adam said. "Even the canoes and kayaks that were pushed up on the sand."

Desi and I looked at each other again and then rushed over to the railing to try to catch a glimpse of the boats in the lake. She grabbed my arm and pointed through the brush to a spot in front of the cabin.

"There's one right there."

Sure enough, there was a bright red kayak drifting aimlessly in the water about twenty feet from the bank. We turned around to face our husbands.

"So somebody did this on purpose?" I couldn't imagine how much time that must have taken to get all of the boats off the beach. I'd been canoeing before and it took some strength to move their weight without the benefit of water buoyancy.

"That's the way it looks." Tomàs stroked his chin. "The

resort staff will have a hard time getting all those boats back."

My stomach rolled. Poor Leah. Was this more of the vandalism they'd referred to? Who could be doing this? I didn't want to say anything in front of Tomàs about the possibility that this was not an isolated incident, because I figured we were already skating on thin ice to be able to stay at the resort after Jed's murder.

"Is there anything we can do to help?" I asked.

Adam poured coffee into his cup from the thermos he'd carried in. "I suppose we can help them round up the boats. We're not going to be getting any fishing in this morning."

"We'll have to find a boat to go out after the rest of them," Tomàs said, staring out at the lake. "I think I saw a boat on the shore of that property over there." He pointed to the far side of the lake, where a small cabin was tucked away amidst a grove of trees.

"Do Del and Leah know about this?" I asked.

"Yes. Del was out on the docks this morning, as surprised as we were."

As I was wondering what help I could possibly be to Leah, a little voice called out from behind me. "Mommy? Why is Anthony here?" Mikey asked me.

Behind him, Anthony leaned against the doorframe, blearily rubbing his eyes.

"Everything's fine, boys." Desi took their hands and led them over to the table. "What would you like for breakfast? I've got toast or Pop-Tarts, or even some of my famous blue-berry muffins."

Mikey's eyes lit up. He slid onto the chair and put his arms on the table. "Blueberry muffins. Yay."

I got them both glasses of milk, while Desi placed muffins on plates and set them in front of the kids.

"Well, I guess everyone's up now." I looked over to Adam. "Maybe we can go find Del and ask how we can help."

"Sure, when the kids are done eating and the babies have been fed, let's go. I'm sure they'll still need our help then."

Once everyone was fed, we made our way over to the lake in a bedraggled processional of adults, toddlers, and the double stroller with the babies in it.

Del and Leah stood at the banks of the lake, conferring. She looked up when we approached them. "So you've heard about the boats."

I nodded. "What can we do to help?"

Her eyes strayed to the dozens of watercraft drifting on the lake. In a tired voice, she said, "We'll have to ask the neighbors for the use of their boats." She turned to Del. "Can you go over to Thompson's Resort and see if they'll let us borrow a few rowboats or something?"

"I can do that." Del eyed Tomàs and Adam. "Would you mind coming with me? We could use all the help we can get."

The men climbed into Del's beat-up red truck, which was parked near the boat ramp, leaving Leah, Desi, me, and the kids behind.

"Well, until they get back with some borrowed boats, there's not much we can do." Leah looked in the direction of the departing truck, bouncing through the scattered potholes in the dirt road. "Would anyone be interested in some coffee and pancakes at the café? My treat."

"Pancakes! I love pancakes," Anthony said. Mikey jumped up and down next to him, apparently forgetting that they had each just consumed a giant blueberry muffin.

I shook my head, a grin spreading across my face.

"Those boys are going to eat us out of house and home eventually."

"I don't think it's too far-off in the future," Desi said. "Last week, Anthony ate half a pepperoni pizza in one sitting." She turned to the kids. "Ok, boys, let's go."

We followed Leah to the café, where she placed an order with the cook for a platter of pancakes and a round of coffee. Leah found the kids some coloring books and crayons while we waited for our food to arrive. Before I knew it, a heaping mound of pancakes appeared in front of us. Mikey grabbed two of them and put them on his plate. Before I could stop him, he'd grabbed the container of syrup and upended it. I managed to extract the pitcher from his hands, but not until he had poured out half of the maple syrup onto his pancakes.

Next to him, Anthony's eyes widened until they were almost as big as the pancakes. "My turn."

I scooted the syrup closer to me, before he could get it too.

"I think Mikey should share some of his syrup with you." I used the fork to spear one of the pancakes and set it on Anthony's plate to distribute some of the syrup.

The three of us adults each ate one pancake apiece, leaving the rest of them for the ravenous boys.

While they were immersed in their sugary treats, I asked, "Do you think that this was done by the same person as the other vandalism that occurred at the resort?"

Desi looked at me quizzically. "What are you talking about? Has this happened before?"

"The other things were all pretty minor." Leah's skin reddened, and she looked down at the table. "We've been trying hard to not let the guests find out about the acts of vandalism. Things like that don't look too good for our business."

"Oh, don't worry about us," Desi said, patting Leah's hand. "We just want to help."

Leah's eyes misted over. "Thank you. You and your husband don't even know me, and you've been so kind."

Desi smiled at her. "We're happy to help. We understand what it's like to have a family business, and unfortunately know firsthand how difficult it can be when tragedy affects your business."

I frowned, thinking of the havoc that had ensued after I'd found a body floating just off the Boathouse's docks. In the first few days after the media firestorm that followed, I'd wondered if my in-laws' event center would make it with all the bad publicity.

"Desi's right, just let us know what we can do."

We finished eating and took the kids over to the playground. Leah joined us, I think because she wanted a distraction. As we watched the boys' antics on the jungle gym, I was happy to at least provide that small comfort to her.

Before too long, the men came back. None of them wore smiles.

"They don't look like they have good news for us," Desi observed.

"Del, were you able to borrow any boats from the Thompsons?" Leah asked.

He shook his head. "Don Thompson said all of them have been rented for the day."

Leah's face clouded over. "What are we going to do?" she whispered. "Our guests that have reserved boats for the day aren't going to be happy."

Del shrugged. "I'll walk along the lakeshore with the

guys and see if there are any boats close enough to swim for."

They left again, leaving us to stare at each other.

"There has to be something else." Desi took a sip of her now cold coffee.

"Isn't there anyone else that might have a boat?" I asked.

Leah pursed her lips. "I can't think of anyone who has a boat, well, who would be willing to let us borrow it."

I'd seen her hesitate. "So is there someone else nearby that has a boat?" I knew that there weren't many developed properties on Thunder Lake. That was one of the big draws of the lake—that it wasn't too crowded. But now, that attractive quality was what was causing us problems.

"Well," she said slowly, "there is one neighbor that has a small fishing boat with an outboard motor." Her face darkened. "But I doubt he'll let us borrow it. He isn't known for being very neighborly, and we've had some run-ins with him in the past."

"We'll just have to change his mind." Desi pushed her plate away. "Let's go find this neighbor and convince him to loan us a boat. We're going to get all of your boats back, Leah."

When we were outside, Leah turned to us and asked, "Are you sure you want to do this? Tyler Shafer isn't the nicest of neighbors."

"Oh, I completely understand. I used to have a dreadful neighbor." As soon as I said it, I regretted it. Mr. Weston hadn't been a great neighbor, but I had felt bad about his death and it seemed wrong to speak ill of him at this point.

Desi seemed to sense my discomfort. "We've got kids in our group, how horrible could he be to us?"

Leah looked across the lake and said, "I guess we'll find out."

We started walking toward the far edge of the resort, near Del's mobile home.

"Do we not need to go along the road to get to this place?" I asked. All I could see in front of us was an endless thicket of trees. How were we going to get through that mess with the double stroller?

Leah pointed to a bend in the lake. "There's a path that runs right along there."

Sure enough, as we rounded the other side of the mobile home, I saw the path that Leah had described. It didn't look well-traveled, but it had seen some use in the recent past.

Leah saw me looking at it. "Jed was friends with Tyler. They hung out sometimes." She amended her statement. "Or rather they went drinking together."

I nodded. Even after his death, there was no love lost between Leah and Del's cousin. The trail along the edges of the lake was just wide enough for Desi's double stroller. Even so, it was slow going as we navigated the tree roots snaking across the pathway. After about a quarter of a mile, we came to a clearing. The tree canopy had opened, revealing a dilapidated barn and the small A-frame cabin I'd seen from the dock. A brand-new silver truck was parked next to the house.

A dog barked, and I told Mikey and Anthony to stand behind me as I searched the property for the dog.

Desi saw it first. She pointed toward the far side of the cabin. "It's over there."

I followed her gaze. A large dog that looked like a mix of every breed of dog that would be outlawed by an apartment complex was chained to the side of the cabin. I sighed in relief. We'd left Goldie in the screened-in porch of our cabin, lazily lounging around in the warm air. I'd briefly considered bringing him along on our visit, but now I was glad that I hadn't. I didn't know how this dog would react to a canine intruder.

I took in the rest of the surroundings. Two overflowing trash cans were situated safely out of reach of the dog. Once upon a time, the cabin must have been beautiful, with rough-hewn cedar logs. Now, the logs were dry and cracked. It appeared that the only thing Tyler cared about was his truck. I wasn't holding out much hope of attaining a usable boat from this guy.

"You're trespassing on my property," a man called out. "Leave now or I'll let my dog loose." He was dressed in a red and black plaid shirt over well-worn jeans. He appeared to be in his forties, but his hair was tipped with silver.

Leah waved at him. "Tyler, it's me, Leah—from the resort."

The man lifted his sunglasses and peered at her. "Oh, you."

Beside me, Desi sighed. Neither of us said anything, and I was happy to let Leah do all the talking with this man.

"You may not have noticed, but all of our boats are loose on the lake." Leah jutted her thumb in the direction of the lake.

He raised his eyebrows and glanced in that direction. "How did that happen?"

"I don't know," Leah said in a tight voice. "But I really wish I knew who did it. Is there any way we could borrow a boat from you? We've got to get them back as soon as possible, but we need to be able to get out there and catch them."

"You wouldn't give me an easement to cross your property and now you want a favor from me?" He laughed harshly.

"Look, I'm sorry about that, but we can't have your

driveway bisecting our hiking trail. It's just not safe for our guests."

"Well, we wouldn't want that, now would we." He shrugged. "I guess you'll just have to worry about getting those boats back some other way because I'm not loaning you my boat. Now, please get off of my property."

"Thank you for your time," Leah said through tight lips. She tugged on my arm. "Let's go."

The dog barked at us as we scurried away down the path leading back to the resort.

When we were safely back on resort grounds, Desi stopped and took a breath. "Wow, he isn't very nice."

Leah smirked. "I told you so. He's been a thorn in our sides since we bought the place."

"So what are you going to do about the loose boats?" I asked.

"I don't know." She appeared to have aged by several years. "I hope Del will be able to figure something out. If not, we'll have to wait until we can get a boat from Thompson's Resort this evening." She glanced at her watch. "I'd better get back to the office. People will be wanting to checkout soon. I'll see you later, ok?"

"Bye," Desi called to Leah as she walked off toward the office.

When Leah was out of sight, Desi said, "Now what? I'd counted on the guys being out all morning fishing. I was kind of looking forward to some time out on the deck."

"Well, they'll still be gone, they'll just be catching boats instead of fish—as long as they can track down one boat to get started." I glanced at the lake. "Let's get the kids back to the cabin and we can decide what to do." The two of us returned to the cabin together to map out the rest of our day.

We played games with the kids until Adam and Tomàs returned. Fortunately, Del had been able to swim out to a rowboat, and between the three of them, they'd recovered all of the boats. After the early morning, everyone was pretty tired and we spent the rest of the day hanging out at the cabins.

12

$\mathcal{T}$he next day, we arranged with the resort for a private guided hike in the hills that rose high above Thunder Lake. Under the canopy of trees, the temperature was pleasant, with just enough spots of sun peeking through the branches to keep us warm. Birds chirped above us, competing with the sound of our hiking boots crunching on dried leaves and moss along the hard-packed dirt trail.

Adam carried Ella in a hiking carrier on his back, and Desi had Lina in a front pack. Tomàs and I wore backpacks containing food, water, and an emergency first aid kit. The boys walked along beside us. I hadn't been sure what to expect, but so far, the hike had exceeded my expectations—that is, with the exception of our guide, Sela.

I'd seen her around the resort, but I hadn't met her until the hike. She was younger than Adam and I, maybe in her mid-twenties. She wore her long dark hair loose around her shoulders and was dressed in a tank top and shorts that barely reached to mid-thigh. Her backpack and well-worn hiking boots were the only nod to a day that would be spent in the woods.

According to Leah, Sela was an experienced hiker in the area and we were in good hands, but I had my doubts. Desi and I had tried to talk with our guide since we'd left the resort, but our questions so far had been met with terse responses. Sela had glared at me so many times that I couldn't help but wonder why she didn't like me.

The hike itself had been fairly easy so far. The trail we were on had gradual changes in elevation for the most part, and the two boys didn't seem to be having any trouble with it. I'd worried that we'd end up having to carry them when they grew tired, but it hadn't been a problem. I was determined not to let Sela's grumpiness affect us, so I tried again to get her to open up to us.

"So, have you lived in this area for long?" I asked her.

"I've been here for a couple of years. I had family in the area, but they've since moved away." She said all of this while looking straight ahead at the trail we were on.

"Oh, you must really like the area if you decided to stay here after they left," Desi observed. "It is beautiful here." She adjusted the straps of the front pack she was carrying Lina in.

Sela shrugged. "The area is nice, I guess, but I decided to stay for other reasons." She turned away from us and quickened her pace.

Desi and I exchanged glances.

"She's not very talkative," I whispered.

"Well, not everybody is a chatterbox like us."

"Haha. I can be quiet sometimes," I said.

"Really?" She smirked at me. "You hate awkward silences."

I was about to respond, but Mikey broke in first.

"Mommy," he said, as he tugged on my arm, "my shoelace came untied again."

I groaned. Not again. "Sela," I called out.

She turned. "Did you need something?"

"Can we stop for a moment? Mikey needs his shoelace tied." I pointed at his feet.

She rolled her eyes, but called out to the men, who were hiking in front of her. "Tomàs, Adam. We're going to stop for a moment."

They stopped to wait.

I leaned down to tie Mikey's shoelace. His hiking boots were the first pair of shoes that I'd ever bought him that had shoelaces instead of Velcro closures, and so far I wasn't liking them. This was the third time that day that I'd had to tie them. Even with a double knot, they kept coming undone.

Adam came over to us. "I think we'll have to get him some new shoelaces before I take him out hiking any harder trails."

"I think so too." I pulled the laces tight and pushed myself up from the ground.

Directly in front of me, a small creature skittered across the path, not two inches from my own hiking boots. I shrieked and jumped back, bumping into Adam.

"Whoa, honey." He leaned against a tree to catch his balance. He peered at me. "Are you ok? Your face is white."

I nodded. "I think so. What was that thing? It looked like a rat."

I hated any animal that even resembled a rodent more than anything in the world. I usually tried to avoid activities that would include being near any such creatures, but I hadn't wanted to miss out on this hike with my family.

Sela stomped up to us. "It was probably just a vole." She smirked at me. "Did it scare you?"

I didn't like her tone. I straightened to my full five-foot, four-inch height, and looked her in the eye. "It startled me."

She laughed, evidently not believing me. "Wait until we get further into the woods, where the brush is heavier. Then you'll see a whole bunch more of those things."

My feet froze in place.

Adam put his hands on my shoulders and whispered into my ear, "Don't worry about it, honey. We'll be right here with you."

I took a deep breath and forced a smile. "I'm sure the rest of the hike will be lovely." I looked down at Mikey. "Are you ready to go?"

"Yep!" He ran ahead to join Anthony, who was investigating a rotten log that lay alongside the path. They poked at something moving on it, most likely a huge colony of ants. We pulled them away from it and walked in silence for a couple of minutes.

Then, Desi asked Sela, "So, how long have you worked here at the resort?" She seemed determined to engage her in conversation.

"Oh, a little over two years. But I probably won't be here much longer."

"Why is that?" Tomàs peered at Sela. She stopped, and we came to a halt around her.

"I probably shouldn't say anything." Judging by the gleeful expression on her face, she didn't mind telling tales out of school. "But the resort will be sold soon, and then I won't really have any reason to be here anymore."

My head reeled back in shock. "What do you mean the resort will be sold soon?" Leah hadn't mentioned anything of the sort. In fact, she'd been talking about the need to keep the resort afloat over the winter, so they could make it into the next summer season.

"Well, you know. Now that Del and Leah are getting divorced, the resort is going to be sold."

"That's not what Leah said." Desi narrowed her eyes at Sela.

"Of course, that's not what she wants. But Del is going to sell the resort. He's been telling her that for months. When the divorce is finalized, Thunder Lake Resort will go on the market."

Leah had omitted that important detail. I knew the resort meant a lot to her. To hear Del tell it, it was the reason for the dissolution of their marriage. I was surprised that Leah didn't seem more upset with Del about his desire to sell the resort. Maybe she was in denial about the whole thing.

"It sounds like you and Del are close." Desi fiddled with the head covering on Lina's carrier, but she didn't take her eyes off of Sela.

I also watched her expression intently.

We were not disappointed. Sela blushed a little at the mention of Del's name.

"We've been friends for a while," she said slyly. "Let's just say that Del is special to me." She started walking again, but said over her shoulder, "He doesn't really want me talking about it, so that's all I can say. Now, this part of the trail is a bit steeper, so watch your step and stay away from the edge."

We followed Sela as we climbed higher up the hill-side. Rounding a corner, we came out at an overlook, high above the lake. The change in elevation altered my perception of the lake. It seemed large from its shores, but from here, it looked no bigger than a duck pond. I searched the trees below, trying to make out the resort buildings.

Sela stood back, picking at her fingernails. She'd implied that she and Del were an item, but I couldn't see what he saw in her. Did Leah know that Sela and Del were involved? I knew they were separated, but it didn't seem like Leah was ready to give up on their marriage yet. Had Sela been a cause of their separation?

"Oh, I see a squirrel." Before I could get to him, Mikey ran over to the edge, his untied shoelaces flapping in the air. His foot caught on one and he pitched forward, falling over the edge of the trail.

My eyes widened in horror.

"Mikey," I screamed. I raced to the spot I'd seen him go over, fearing the worst. Everyone else rushed over to the side as well. I surveyed the brush-covered embankment, but I didn't see my son. Icy fear shot through every vein in my body.

"Mikey?" Anthony whimpered from next to me.

Desi grabbed him and pulled him away from the edge. "Come on, let's go wait for them over here."

"Mommy?" A faint voice floated up from below us.

I could just make out Mikey's tousled blond hair emerging from the side of a large bush about ten feet down the steep hillside.

"Mikey, stay there. I'm coming to get you." Adam swung Ella's carrier off his back and shoved the hiking backpack at me. He scrambled over the edge, sand and pebbles skittering down below him as he dislodged sediment with each foothold.

"That's not safe to do," Sela called down to him.

He glanced up at her, while holding onto a tree root. "I

don't really care about safety right now—that's my son down there."

"I don't recommend it," Sela said again.

I wanted to wrap my hands around her throat, but instead, Tomàs and I just ignored her. Mikey needed us to focus on him.

"Daddy," Mikey whimpered, "I don't know if I can hold on much longer." His hands looked so small, gripping a tree root as he clung to the side of the cliff.

"It's ok, sweetie, Daddy's almost there. We love you," I shouted to him. My voice trembled and I bit my lip, trying not to let Mikey see me cry.

"Hang on, Mikey, I'm almost there," Adam said.

"Ok." Mikey rested his head against the dirt in front of him.

"Adam. There's a little ledge to your left," Tomàs called out, his eyes darting around, trying to give Adam good instructions on descending the steep incline.

Adam's foot shifted over and found purchase on the ledge. He was now only a few feet away from Mikey.

"Ok, Mikey, when I get down to you, I'm going to help you up onto the ledge." Adam climbed down to a smaller, lower ledge just above Mikey's head. He leaned down, offering our son his hand. "Grab onto my hand, I've got you."

Mikey nodded and gripped Adam's hand. Adam pulled him up, setting him down on the wide spot just above him. Mikey's face was ashen and blood trickled down his arm from a network of scrapes.

I had never been so scared in my entire life, even when I had a gun pointed directly at my face.

"I'm going to need you to climb up in front of me. I'll be

right behind you. It's just like the climbing wall at the playground, and I know you're going to do a great job at it. You're my little monkey." Adam rested his hand on Mikey's back. Mikey nodded, a determined expression coming over his face.

"Ready?" Adam asked, patting Mikey's leg.

He nodded and started climbing. Only a few minutes later, his head appeared above the side. Tomàs leaned down to grab his little arms and Adam pushed him up the final few feet, then climbed up himself, sitting for a moment next to our son—finally safe.

I rushed over to them, tears streaming down my face. I grabbed Mikey in my arms and buried my face in his hair, pulling him tightly to me. I was shaking so much that Mikey pulled away and asked, "Mommy, are you ok?"

I blinked back my tears and smiled weakly at him. "I'm ok, honey. I was just so worried about you."

"I'm ok, Mommy." He stood and offered me his hands. Adam pushed himself up from the ground as well, and we joined Desi, Tomàs, and Anthony where they stood safely away from the edge. They huddled around us, everyone's voices giddy with happiness that this hadn't ended in tragedy.

Sela stood off to the side. "That's why I told you not to go so close to the edge."

We all stared at her.

She shifted uncomfortably. "Do you want to continue this hike?"

I shook my head rapidly. "No way. We're going back to the cabin right now."

The others agreed, and we made our way back down the trail to the resort. After we reached our cabin, I collapsed into a chair on the deck, my knees so wobbly that they were no longer able to hold me. I felt as though every ounce of energy had been drained from my body.

The boys were playing inside the cabin, acting as if nothing had happened. I don't think they even realized how much danger Mikey had been in. Or at least, as little kids, they had quickly forgotten. That was probably for the best, as I didn't want their vacation to be ruined. I, however, would never forgive myself for allowing myself to get distracted and not watching Mikey more carefully. I vowed that this would be the best vacation ever, even with all of its mishaps. Nothing was more important to me than my family.

13

----

*A*dam and I spent the afternoon with the kids in our cabin, playing as many games of Candy Land with Mikey as he wanted. I kept kissing Mikey and hugging him close to me. We'd come way too close to losing him.

I wanted to stay with my family all afternoon, but I still needed to coordinate with Del for the Labor Day celebration on the upcoming weekend. Del was in charge of the boat races and I'd volunteered to run the other events. I had the medal for the winner of the boat race and ribbons for all of the other activities, but I wanted to confirm that all the items we'd need for the games—like a rope, spoons, eggs, and ties—would be available.

Mikey drew a card with a yellow square on it and moved his playing piece ahead to the next yellow space. I chose my card next and noticed Mikey rubbing his eyes. I nudged Adam.

"I think it's time for someone's nap," I whispered.

He nodded. "How about we finish up this game and then we all take a nap?"

Mikey looked like he wanted to protest, but instead he yawned. "Ok, Daddy."

Usually he wouldn't want to take a nap, insisting that he wasn't tired, but the adrenaline had worn off from his ordeal out on the trail. When the game was done and we declared Mikey the winner, he dutifully crawled into his twin bed in the other room. Adam set Ella in her Pack 'n Play next to him and they both fell asleep instantly.

"Now what?" Adam eyed his book on the end table.

"Go ahead and read it. If you don't mind, I need to talk to Del about a few things for this weekend."

"Yeah, no problem. While you're gone, I'll try to figure out what we want for dinner."

"Thanks, honey." I gave him a big hug. "It shouldn't take long."

He waved at me and then settled down in the comfy chair in the living area to read his favorite author's latest thriller. When he'd been a corporate attorney, he hadn't had much time for his own hobbies, so it was nice to see him enjoying life again.

I wasn't sure where I'd find Del, so I tried knocking on the door of his mobile home first. No one answered, so I turned around to survey the resort. From here, I could see a great deal of the area, but not everything. I didn't see Del.

After checking the boathouse and the garden shed near the campfire pit, I finally found him weeding the flower beds next to the office.

"Ah, so you're the one with the green thumb." I jutted my thumb at the hanging flower pots.

He smiled and stood, running a rake over the immaculate flower beds to capture any stray weeds. "Yes. My mother always had a huge flower garden when I was a kid, and I guess it rubbed off on me. I love competing with myself every year to see how big the flowers in the hanging baskets can grow."

"They're beautiful." I admired the hanging baskets once again. Bees buzzed around the giant blossoms cascading over the sides of the pots. I'm sure Adam would be jealous of Del's green thumb if he saw them. "I bet you'll miss them when you sell the resort."

He seemed taken aback. "How did you know I wanted to sell the resort? I didn't think Leah wanted to admit it was a possibility, much less tell people about it."

I shrugged. "Sela told us today when were out on a hike with her."

He grimaced and clutched the handle of the rake tighter.

"Ah. I should have known."

For someone who supposedly was in a relationship with Sela, he didn't appear too fond of her.

"This probably isn't any of my business, but does Leah know you're dating Sela?" I watched him closely.

His face fell. "I wouldn't say I'm dating her. We were both out at Rex's Place last week and ended up sitting next to each other at the bar. I may have had too much to drink and said more to her than I should have." He sighed. "It was nice having a woman's attention, but I shouldn't have led her on. Leah always said Sela had a thing for me."

"So you do want to sell the resort?"

He leaned on the rake handle. "It's not so much that I want to sell the resort, but more that I can't be here anymore."

"Can't?

"Remember what Leah was like back in Seattle? She was so fun and lively." His face twisted wistfully.

I nodded. "I do." She'd been so entertaining to be around and I had fond memories of spending time with her after work at happy hour every Friday. "So how do you think coming out here changed her?"

"She became obsessed with the resort. I know I'm the one that talked her into buying the property in the first place, but once she was out here, she lived and breathed the resort. There wasn't any time left for me."

"She mentioned you'd been having some financial difficulties with the resort."

He gazed out toward the lake. "The hospitality industry is never easy. We had so many customers cancel their reservations last year when we had those big forest fires in the area—not that I blame them. If I could have left then, I would have too. The smoke was horrible." He sighed. "We never quite recovered from that and have been playing catch-up on bills ever since."

"So selling the resort makes the most sense."

"It does business-wise, but unless I force the sale, I don't think Leah will ever realize that." Sadness crossed his face. "Jed wanted me to sell the resort and join him in a business venture—start fresh somewhere else."

"Oh?" I didn't say much, allowing him room to talk.

"My cousin had come into some money recently from a past business, and he wanted us to pool our money and open a bar or something back home in North Dakota."

My heart lurched in my chest. Was Jed's past business venture a cover for ill-gotten gains from the jewelry store robbery? The more I learned about him, the more I wondered if there was some merit to my crazy theory that he'd robbed the store.

"Wow. That would be different." I peered at him. "Do you think you'll do that now?"

"Nah. It was more Jed's thing. Besides, I won't get enough

proceeds from the sale of the resort to buy a car, much less a bar."

"I'm sorry for your loss. It sounds like you and he were quite close." I already knew that from Leah, but I wanted to hear what Del would say.

"We were. The two of us were all that remained of our family. Now, I guess I'm the only one left."

"Do the police know anything yet about who could have killed him?"

"Not that I know." He toed the ground with the tip of his sneaker then looked up at me. "You probably came to find me for some reason. Did you need something from me?"

I smiled. "I wanted to touch base with you about the celebration this weekend. Is everything set with the boats for the race now that you've got them all back?"

He nodded. "Everything should be on track. I've got the tug-of-war rope all cleaned up. It was pretty dirty from lying in a heap in the shed for the last year. And everything else should be easy to set up. We need a couple dozen eggs for the spoon race and a few other things, but the catering is the biggest thing. Leah said you were taking over that part of the celebration. Did you get everything sorted out with the restaurant in town that's catering?"

"I have a few more things to check on, but so far, so good."

"Great." He looked up at the sky. "It's going to be a hot one today. I'd better get this done before it gets too horrible." He motioned to the gardens that stretched around the side of the office.

"Sure, sure. I'll let you get to it."

He started raking the gravel away from the decorative edging on the flower bed. I walked away slowly, thinking about what he'd said. It didn't sound like he was dating anyone else and he seemed to miss Leah—or rather the person she'd been before they moved to the resort. I didn't blame him. I'd seen a change in my old friend as well. I admired her passion for the resort, but I wondered if it had become too all-consuming for her.

I returned to our cabin. I heard Lina crying next door, but our cabin was silent. I tiptoed in past Adam and checked on the kids—still sound asleep. In the living room, I flopped down on the hide-a-bed couch.

Adam looked up from his book. "Did you get everything worked out?"

I nodded.

"Good." He smiled at me. "If you need help with any of it, let me know. I'm sure Tomàs and Desi are up for helping too."

"Thanks." I regarded him. "I really appreciate you supporting me on this. I know this is supposed to be our vacation and now I'm working for part of it."

He shrugged. "Leah's your friend and she needs help. I'd do the same if it were my friend."

A rush of love came over me and I walked over to him, kissing him squarely on the mouth. He looked at me in surprise.

"What was that for?"

"For being such a good husband."

He winked at me and said, "I'll have to be good more often."

To that, I slugged him in the arm and he laughed, closing his book.

"Did you think about what we'd have for dinner?" I asked.

"Desi came over and said Anthony had been begging for

roasted hot dogs. Is that ok with you? We can roast them out in that small fire pit in front of our cabins."

I mentally assessed our food provisions. "If she's got hot dogs and buns, that's fine with me."

"I think she does, but you might want to check."

"I'll go ask her," I said as I walked toward the door.

Over at their cabin, Desi was pacing their deck, gently bouncing Lina in her arms.

"I can't get her to sleep."

Lina scrunched up her face and let out a cry in response to her mother's proclamation.

"Do you want me to try?" I held out my arms for my niece.

"Sure." Desi handed her over. "Tomàs and Anthony are napping inside, and I didn't want to wake them up."

In my arms, Lina cried softly a little, then settled down and fell asleep.

"Seriously?" Desi said. "I've been trying for hours. You're like the baby whisperer."

I rocked Lina in my arms. "She was probably just about to give up. Maybe having someone else take her helped."

"Well, I don't really care at this point, I just wanted her to sleep." Desi fell into a chair and rested her head against the back of it. "Ah, this is nice."

I laughed and sat down in the chair next to her, being careful not to move Lina too much.

"Adam said you wanted to roast hot dogs for dinner."

She made a face. "I didn't say that. I said Anthony wants to. I'm not a fan. But we brought the fixings with us, so I couldn't say no."

"How about we suffer through the hot dogs and then get something we want in town tomorrow while the boys are out fishing?"

"Works for me." She turned to face me. "Adam said you were out talking to Del?"

"Yeah, I needed to confirm a few things for the Labor Day celebration with him." A bird squawked in the tree next to the deck, distracting me for a moment.

"Did you ask him about that witch, Sela?" She leaned forward.

"I did. He said they were never dating—not that she wasn't interested in him. I think he still has feelings for Leah."

"Which explains why Sela hates Leah's friends so much. Still, her behavior today wasn't very professional. You should really tell Leah about what happened with Mikey."

I sighed. "I might, but I don't want to stir up any more drama than there already is. I thought this vacation would be more relaxing."

Desi laughed. "There's always something. I think you'd be bored if everything went according to plan."

Over at our cabin, I heard Ella crying.

"I'd better get back over there. Hot dogs out front at five?"

"Works for me."

I carefully handed Lina back to her mother and went back to attempt a second try at being a baby whisperer.

14

That night, they started up the bonfire again for s'mores—to create a sense of normalcy, I guessed —but we didn't attend. I wasn't sure that I could be there after finding Jed's body at the fire pit. We fell asleep with the faint odor of smoke drifting in through the windows along with the fresh pine-scented air. It wasn't entirely unpleasant and reminded me of all of the happy times I had had camping in the past.

When I woke in the middle of the night and got up to check on the kids, the smell of smoke was stronger. I stood still, sniffing the air. The fire should have been out hours ago. What was going on?

I pushed aside the curtains in our room and looked out the window. Above our cabin, a fire blazed in the fire pit. I hastily put on a sweatshirt and my flip-flops and rushed out the door. I couldn't think of any reason why there would be a fire going at this time of night.

I reached the fire pit and stopped short. Luckily, this time there weren't any bodies, but the flames were consuming something that wasn't logs. What looked to be every single life jacket that the resort owned had been piled in the middle of the fire pits and set ablaze. An empty gas can had been left near the edge of the graveled area and the scent of gasoline filled the air, competing with the smoke.

My eyes darted around, but I saw no one in the area. I needed to tell Del or Leah. Her house was closer, so I ran over to it and pounded on the door. The lights were off, and she must've been sleeping. I knocked again. Finally, a light came on and I heard footsteps in the house coming toward me. Leah flung the door open.

"Jill, what are you doing here?" She pulled her pink bathrobe closer against her body and folded her arms across her chest. "Is something wrong?"

I tried to catch my breath and then responded, "Somebody set all of the life jackets on fire."

Her eyebrows shot up and her voice became elevated. "Where?"

"In the fire pits. It looks like they used gasoline."

Her face blanched. "I was hoping that whoever was doing this would stop." She turned away from me and said over her shoulder, "I'll call Del." She disappeared for a minute or two and then came out, wearing a sweatshirt and a pair of sweatpants.

We hurried back to the fire, with which was still burning brightly. Flames licked at the pile of blue and red life vests, sending plumes of black smoke into the air. Del ran up to us from the direction of his mobile home, wearing only a short sleeve shirt and jeans.

He assessed the situation and kicked the gasoline can far away from the fire. "We've got to get this thing put out before anyone else sees it." He ran over to the shed to retrieve a hose, which he hooked up near the fire, directing the water at the flames.

When there was nothing left but smoldering pieces of what used to be life jackets, Del and Leah stared at the fire, their arms hanging limply by their sides.

"Del," she said softly.

"I know. We have to figure out who's doing this. This is getting out of hand." He closed his eyes for a moment and ran his fingers through his hair. "Did they burn all of the life jackets? Those things are expensive."

"I don't think so. But it's so dark that it's hard to tell." Leah motioned to the boathouse. "Let's check and see."

I wasn't sure that I should be a part of this, but I was already involved, so I followed them down to the lake.

When we reached the boathouse, Del reached out and grabbed the lock, then dropped it as though it had burned his hand.

"This wasn't cut. Whoever did this knew the combination." We all stared at the combination lock, hanging forlornly from a metal loop on the open door.

"So if it wasn't cut, it must've been one of our staff." Leah leaned against the side of the boathouse and put her head in her hands.

"I suppose someone could have left it unlocked, but yeah, it's most likely someone who works here." Del patted her awkwardly on the shoulder. He opened the door fully, revealing the racks where they kept the life jackets. Although one of the racks was still full, the other was empty. Somebody had burned half of the resort's supply of life jackets.

For a while, we just looked at the empty rack, none of us saying anything. Finally, Del said, "I'll take care of cleaning out the fire pit. We don't want the guests to see that." He shivered in the cool air.

"You should put a coat on if you're going to be out here much longer," Leah said, her face full of concern.

He frowned. "Jed was wearing my coat the day he died. He couldn't find his, so I said he could borrow mine." Tears pooled in the corners of his eyes, but he glanced at the lake and composed himself. "I haven't had time to get a new one yet."

Leah and I nodded.

"I'd better get going." He turned abruptly and stalked off toward the garden shed, leaving us standing in the doorway of the boathouse.

"I'm so sorry, Leah. This is just horrible." I shivered. The breeze coming off the lake was freezing cold. I hadn't planned on being outside for this long, so I was only wearing light clothing.

She looked up at me with teary eyes. "At first we thought it was a joke, but this isn't funny. Somebody is doing this with malicious intent. Replacing the vandalized items could ruin us financially." She pushed her hair back away from her head. "Do you think we should sell the resort?"

My eyes locked with hers. I didn't know what to say. I knew how important the resort was to her, and I didn't want to sway her in either direction. "Is selling the resort what you want?"

She shook her head. "No." The tears fell quicker now and she looked up at me. "Del wants to sell the resort. I didn't want to tell you, because I was hoping I could change his mind. With everything that's happened in the last week, I don't think that's going to happen."

I gave her a hug.

"This probably isn't the right time to make such a major decision." I motioned to the lock. "Maybe we should lock up and go back to your house. It sounds like Del is going to take care of the fire pit, and there's nothing you can really do until tomorrow morning anyway. You might as well get some rest."

She bobbed her head slowly. "Thanks, Jill. I'm glad you were here this week. I don't know if I could deal with this without having someone here to lean on. I think that's what I miss most about separating from Del—now I'm all alone."

I reached out and squeezed her hand. We walked back to her house, and I watched as she went in safely, locking the door behind her. The sun was rising and the birds were stirring, but I was exhausted. I hoped the kids wouldn't wake up for a few more hours so I could get in some shut-eye.

As luck would have it, when I got back into the cabin, everyone was still sound asleep. I crawled into bed next to Adam and snuggled up against him. I tried to sleep, but my attention kept shifting to the open window next to the bed. Someone had set that fire, close to where we slept, similarly to Jed's murder earlier in the week. If I hadn't been made uncomfortable by the close proximity of his murder before, having this happen made me nervous. Who was trying to shut down the resort? And why? How did Jed's murder fit into all of this?

The questions spun around in my tired brain. But, much as I'd advised Leah, there was nothing I could do about it until the morning. I forced myself to close my eyes, and soon fell asleep, though my dreams were filled with images of burning life jackets.

∽

When I woke up the next morning, I could still smell the stale odor of smoke. I lifted a section of my hair and discovered the culprit. Eww. Everyone else was still asleep, so I hopped in the shower and let the water rinse away my worries—well, as much as it could. I wasn't sure if I should tell Adam about the burned life jackets. The vandalism hadn't hurt me and it wasn't my story to tell, so I decided not to tell him. We needed to get on with our family vacation and enjoy the few days we had left at the resort.

We spent the day playing in the sand and swimming in the lake. Mikey and Anthony loved the large floats I'd brought with, making me glad I'd spent the extra time to find them. When they came back up onto the beach to dry off in the sun, I excused myself to make a phone call to check on things back home.

Mikey's school registration was weighing heavily on my mind and I hoped Danielle would be available to answer my call this time. But first, I wanted to check in with Beth about things at the Boathouse and with Fluffy. Last time I'd talked with her, she'd sounded stressed-out with the plans for the upcoming Halloween haunted house. It was my project and I hated that she was stuck dealing with Angela Laveaux while I was on vacation.

The phone rang several times on Beth's end, but no one answered. I ended up leaving a brief message and telling her I'd try to call back later. Next, I tried Danielle. This time, she picked up and my spirits lifted. Finally, I'd be able to get the whole registration mess fixed.

"Hi, Danielle, it's Jill, Mikey Andrews' mom." The springy coil of the pay phone clinked as it hit the sides of the phone booth.

"Oh, hi, Jill. What can I do for you?"

"Well, I spoke with Nancy late last week and she said we'd missed the registration deadline for Mikey to attend Busy Bees this year."

"Oh." She was silent for a moment. "That is true."

I held my breath.

"But there should be room for one more in the pre-kindergarten class. Why don't you give Nancy a call at the school and tell her I said to add Mikey in."

I exhaled. Thank goodness. I felt as though as huge part of what was weighing me down had now been lifted. But I had to talk to Nancy about it? That didn't sound fun.

"Um. I need to call Nancy to do that?" Danielle usually handled such things, so I was surprised she was passing it off to Nancy.

"I'm at Disney World right now," she said. "I don't have my computer with me. Nancy is holding down the fort at the preschool while I'm on vacation."

Of course. It was just my luck that she was across the country from us when I needed her to be in office. Then again, I couldn't fault her for taking a vacation before the school year started—we were doing the same thing.

"That's so cool. I hope you're having fun. We were thinking of taking the kids there in a few years."

"It is nice. It's in the nineties and way more humid than at home, but the palm trees are gorgeous and the kids are having a ball."

I heard a lot of noise in the background on her side.

"Jill, I've got to get going, it's almost our turn to ride Space Mountain."

"Of course. Have fun. I'll see you in a few weeks."

I returned the phone to its cradle and stared blankly at the device. I didn't want to have to call Nancy, especially after how she'd acted when I saw her at the BeansTalk. She'd implied that I was a bad parent for not remembering the registration deadline. I wasn't a bad parent—just a busy one, but I knew that when I called her about registering Mikey, she wasn't going to make it easy.

With dread in my heart, I found the school's number in my phone's address book and punched each number into the pay phone. As much as I wanted to get Mikey's school situation settled, I found myself hoping she wouldn't pick up.

"Busy Bees Preschool," Nancy chirped. "How may I help you?"

I didn't say anything at first and she repeated her question.

"Hello? Is anyone there?"

I cleared my throat. "Sorry, I had a bad connection. This is Jill Andrews. I called Danielle about Mikey's registration and she said to have you add him to the pre-kindergarten class."

"Oh, really? I thought that class was full."

I gritted my teeth. "She said it was fine to add Mikey to it. Is there anything else you need from me right now?"

"No, that's fine. But I'll need you to mail in your registration form as soon as possible—you know, the one that we sent out that had the deadline printed at the top of it?"

I clenched the phone cord so hard that the metal coils left imprints on the skin of my palm. This had been a fun day spent in the sun with my family and I wasn't going to let her ruin it. "Thanks for the reminder. I'll do that as soon as I can."

"You're welcome." The phone clicked and I hung up, resisting the urge to smash something with the heavy phone. I couldn't wait until Mikey was old enough for kindergarten. I supposed I could try to get him into another preschool, but we liked Busy Bees, it was close to our house, and most of all, Anthony went there as well. For Mikey's sake, I'd have to suck it up and play nice with Nancy for at least another year.

I walked back to the lake and forced a smile onto my face.

"Did everything go ok?" Desi asked.

I smiled. "Yes. I forgot to sign Mikey up for preschool for this year, which Nancy oh so nicely reminded me of when I was at the café on Sunday."

"Ouch." She winced. "I saw her talking to you, but things were so busy that day, I didn't get a chance to ask you about it."

"Well, everything is good now. Mikey will be in Anthony's class again and I'll have another year dealing with Nancy." On second thought, maybe it would have been better if Mikey didn't attend Busy Bees.

"I'm glad it all worked out. They send so many pieces of paper and forms home every day—it's a wonder I didn't forget too." She shuddered. "I have mounds of paper at my house on seemingly every surface."

"Me too. But enough talk about Nancy and preschool. This is our vacation!" I clapped my hands and slipped off my sandals. "Now boys, how about we build a sandcastle together?"

They ran off down to their sand toys and I followed them. The lake shone like glittering diamonds in the sun and a gentle heat rose off the sand, warming my bare feet as I walked. You couldn't get much better than this.

15

*L*eah had asked me not to tell anyone about what had happened to the life vests, so on Saturday morning when Adam and Tomàs took the boys out on the lake to teach them how to fish, I didn't say anything to them about it. I hadn't decided yet whether or not I would tell Adam, but my husband's early departure from the cabin gave me a little time to think about it.

While the guys were gone, Desi and I decided to take a trip into town with the babies for groceries. We piled into my minivan and drove along the winding roads to town. I could feel Desi's eyes on me as soon as we left the resort.

"Something's bothering you." She peered at me from the passenger seat.

I tightened my grip on the steering wheel. Desi knew me too well. I didn't want to alarm her by telling her about the vandalism, but I didn't want to lie to her either. Besides, in the past, she'd been a great sounding board when things were bothering me.

I took a deep breath. "Last night, someone took half of

the life vests from the boathouse and burned them in the fire pit above our cabins."

Out of the corner of my eye, I saw her jaw drop.

"That's a lot of life jackets."

I nodded. "It is. I think Leah and Del are going to have to report this one to their insurance company."

"And this all happened when we were sleeping right there in the cabins." Desi's fears echoed mine.

"Yes." I fixed my eyes on the road while Desi processed this information.

"Was it the same person who set all the boats free on the lake? Do you think this had anything to do with Jed's murder?"

I didn't know how to answer her. Boats being set free on the lake was a far cry from killing someone. I supposed Jed could've caught whoever was doing it and they killed him for that but it seemed a little extreme to me.

"I don't know."

"Tomàs told me the local police think someone from Jed's past was responsible for his death. Do you think that isn't true?" She twisted in her seat to look at me full on. "And if it wasn't someone from his past, who did it?"

"It could've been anyone who had access to the resort. I hate to say it, but I've even thought that it may have been Leah." I bit my lip and stared straight ahead. Even so, when Desi gasped, I could feel her reaction to my announcement.

"Leah? Why would she want to kill Del's cousin?"

"She didn't like Jed very much, and he was trying to take Del away from the resort to start up a new business. Apparently Del wanted to sell the resort, and Leah was trying to convince him otherwise." I thought back to what Del had said about Jed taking over his morning watering duties the morning he'd been killed and a chill shot through me. "It was supposed to be Del out there that morning. And Jed had borrowed Del's jacket. What if whoever killed him thought it was Del?"

We were on a straight stretch of road, so I glanced over at Desi. She was looking at me thoughtfully.

"He was speared through the back," she said slowly. "I suppose there could've been a case of mistaken identity. But that still leaves us wondering who killed him."

We passed the sign for the town limits and I lowered the van's speed. I drove past the jewelry store and the ice cream shop where we'd stopped the day we came to the resort. I pulled into a parking spot in the general store's lot.

"Do you think it could have been Leah that killed Jed because she assumed it was Del? Did the resort mean that much to her?" Desi asked as she unbuckled her seatbelt.

I didn't really want to think that my friend could be capable of murdering her husband's cousin, much less her husband himself. "I suppose she could have, but it doesn't seem like her."

"It's been a while since you last saw her."

"I know." I opened my door and the sliding door to the back so we could get the babies out of their car seats. Six years ago, Leah and I had worked together and had so much in common. Now, my life was filled by my children and she'd developed a passion for managing a lakeside resort. I'd once considered her a good friend, but had things changed so much that I no longer knew Leah?

Desi and I shopped for a while, putting the items that needed to keep cold in the ice chest we'd brought along.

"Do you want to stop for lunch?" Desi asked. "It's almost one o'clock."

My stomach rumbled. In worrying about everything happening at the resort, I'd almost forgotten it was lunchtime. "I saw a hamburger joint up the road there—I think they had outdoor seating by the river."

Desi nodded. "Sounds fun."

We got back into the van and I piloted it to the location where I'd seen the drive-in. We ordered our burgers, fries, and milkshakes from the walk-up window, and took them to eat at a picnic table overlooking the river. At this time of year, the river wasn't exactly roaring, but there was still enough water in it to make the view scenic. A few older kids had made their way down the slope and were skipping from rock to rock, laughing as they navigated the slippery surfaces.

"Having someone murdered at the resort and now the vandalism can't be good for the business." Desi munched on a fry and gazed out at the river.

"No, Leah said she thinks they'll lose a lot of business from this. And from what she said, they can't afford to lose any more money on the resort. She's starting to wonder herself if they should sell."

"That will be awful if she's forced to sell," Desi said. "I know how difficult it can be to have the public's eye on you and have it affecting business."

"No kidding, I thought we would never get over having a body found at the Boathouse. With all of those cancellations, it seemed like it would be years before we could recover from the bad publicity. Luckily, things seem to have rebounded faster than I assumed they would."

Desi checked on Lina in her stroller, and then looked at me. "You've got to figure out how to help your friend. I don't know her very well, but I can tell how much the resort means to her. Losing it this way would devastate her."

I took a big bite of my cheeseburger to allow myself time

to think. After swallowing, I said, "If we're going to assume it wasn't Leah who killed Jed, who could it have been?"

"Well, I don't know about you, but I'm not a big fan of Sela." Desi scrunched up her face.

I laughed. She was right. After Mikey's accident, Sela had been incredibly unsympathetic, and considering how cold she'd been, I wouldn't put it past her to kill someone.

"What motive would she have though? It didn't sound like she really knew Jed very well."

"Yeah, but remember how she feels about Del? Those googly eyes she made when she talked about him?" Desi wiggled her eyebrows. "I don't think she'd mind if Del was no longer operating a business with his soon-to-be ex-wife."

"So you think she would've killed Jed just so the resort would fail?"

Desi shrugged. "I don't know, it was just an idea. We were trying to figure out who could've done it, and she's the nastiest person I've encountered here."

"There is something else," I said slowly. How would Desi react if I told her I thought Jed may have robbed the jewelry store in town? If we wanted to help Leah though, I needed to be completely honest about any possibility.

"Jed may have stolen the diamonds from the jewelry store here in town."

"What?" Desi stared at me. "That seems a little far-fetched."

I shrugged. "I know. But when I was looking for information about the celebration, I found an empty velvet jewelry bag on the floor of his closet. Why else would it be there?"

"There could be a million reasons why he had that bag. He hadn't even been living there long—it could have belonged to someone else."

"True, but Tomàs told us Jed had been involved with

some sketchy people in the past. Who's to say that he didn't continue a life of crime while he was in Pemberton."

"I guess so." Desi twisted her napkin around her fingers. "Did they say what the suspects looked like?"

"I don't know. I haven't read the local newspaper or anything. The people I overheard talking didn't mention it."

"Wouldn't the news coverage of it be online?" Desi asked.

"In a small town like this?" I scoffed. "This would have made the front cover of the local paper."

"So, let's see if we can find that out. It just happened, so it should be in the current week's paper." Desi crumpled up her wrappers. "Let's go find out."

I smiled. When Desi got an idea in her head, there was no talking her out of it.

I picked up my garbage and threw it in a nearby trash-can. Holding out my keys, I jingled them in question.

"Where do you think we should try first?"

"Maybe the library?" She pushed Lina's stroller back to the car and we got the girls situated in their car seats.

I drove us back into town, stopping in front of the library. We entered the building and approached the librarian sitting behind the information desk.

She leaned forward, her hands folded in front of her on the desk. "What can I do for you girls?" She eyed us over glasses perched on the tip of her nose.

"We're visiting town and thought it would be nice to get a copy of the local newspaper." Desi smiled sweetly at her. "Do you know where we could get one?"

"Oh, I'm sorry, but we don't have a local newspaper. *The Gazette* shut down a few years ago. Not enough people in this town wanted to read a local paper."

My hopes deflated like a balloon losing helium. I'd

thought finding out what the suspects looked like might help us figure out whether or not it could have been Jed that robbed the jewelry store.

"Thank you for your time," I said.

"Yes, thank you," Desi echoed.

We left the air-conditioned coolness of the library and stood outside next to an oak tree.

"Now what?" Desi asked, while pushing the stroller back and forth to soothe Lina. "We could see if the robbery was big enough to make any online news outlets."

I held Ella in my arms, and she blew bubbles at people passing by us. What were we going to do? Now that I'd brought up the velvet bag, I wanted to track down that lead. Maybe the jewelry store had reopened.

I looked Desi in the eye. "Let's skip the online research and go directly to the source—the jewelry store."

"And what—ask them flat out what the suspects looked like?" She scrunched up her face. "That won't seem odd or anything for tourists to be asking about that."

"I was thinking we could bring it up gradually. Maybe do some jewelry shopping first and then work the conversation around to the robbery?"

"I guess. We don't have many other options."

We walked along Main Street to Junell Jewelers, stopping outside to peruse the window display.

"That heart-shaped diamond necklace is beautiful," Desi said, eying it. "I wish Tomàs would get me something like that for our anniversary. But he's always so practical. I'll probably get a laundry basket instead."

I tilted my head to the side. "Really, Desi? A laundry basket? He's not that bad."

"No? You do remember the vacuum he got me last year for Christmas, right?"

"You asked for that!"

"So?" She pouted a little. "I didn't mean for my only present."

"Well, here's your chance to dream a little." I tugged on her arm and pulled her into the store.

A woman behind the counter looked up when the bells on the door tinkled. "Hello, ladies. It's a nice day out, isn't it?" she said pleasantly.

"It is," I agreed. Desi and I peered into the glass cases.

"Oh my, what beautiful little girls," she said, admiring Ella and Lina, who were both now sleeping in the stroller. "They look like little angels, sleeping so peacefully in there."

I smiled. "Thank you."

"Are you looking for anything in particular?"

"We're in the area on vacation and we thought we'd browse in here while we're in town," I said.

"My anniversary is coming up and I'm thinking my husband could use some suggestions for a present. He gave me a vacuum for Christmas last year. Can you believe that?" Desi said with indignation.

The saleswoman's mouth formed an "o" and her eyes widened. "Wow. Yes. I think he could use some suggestions. What were you thinking about?"

"There's a beautiful heart-shaped necklace in the window. Could I see it a little closer up?"

"Of course." The woman crossed the room to the window and used a key hanging from a chain around her neck to open the case. She brought it over to the counter and laid it down on a piece of velvet cloth the same shade of midnight blue as the bag I'd seen in Jed's closet.

Desi touched it reverently. "It's gorgeous."

"Do you want to try it on?"

Desi nodded and the woman came around to our side of

the counter and clasped it around Desi's neck.

"Ooh," Desi said, viewing herself in the mirror on the counter. "I've got to tell Tomàs about this."

"How long are you in town for?" the saleswoman asked.

"For a few more days. We're staying at the Thunder Lake Resort."

"Ah, I've heard of it." She unclasped the necklace and laid it back down on the cloth. "Have you been staying there long?"

"Since Sunday night," I said. My pulse quickened. This seemed like the perfect opening. "Actually, we were in town when all the police were here. I heard someone say that the store had been robbed."

She gave a slight nod and I shot her a sympathetic look. "That must have been awful."

"It was." She leaned over the counter. "We're not really supposed to talk about it, but I was there that day. The robber drove right into the back of the store and grabbed the diamonds from Mr. Junell's workshop before any of us had a chance to react." She shook her head. "He's well-known for his designs, both locally and throughout the state, and someone had just sent him those diamonds to use in a necklace and bracelet set." She sighed. "I saw his design. They would have been stunning."

"Oh wow." Desi's eyes widened. "So whoever it was crashed into the store."

"Uh huh." She looked around, then locked the necklace in the case below the counter and beckoned for us to follow her to the back of the store. She opened the door to the back, revealing a room that was under construction. "He drove a truck into the door, right there." She pointed. "Mr. Junell was so upset and not just because of the diamonds. He'd recently completed a remodel of the whole back of the store and everything was destroyed when the truck ran into it."

The wall had been blasted out, although a makeshift wall and door had taken its place.

"So the robber was a man?" Desi asked.

"Well, I don't know for sure. The person had one of those knit face masks on, but the way he walked was more like how a man walks, you know?" She closed the door and led us back over to the counter. "For all we know, there could have been a whole group of them, but I only saw one."

Desi and I exchanged glances. If the robber had been Jed, was he in cahoots with someone else?

"Well, I'm glad that this necklace wasn't stolen," Desi said, pointing to the display case in front of us. "It's gorgeous, and my husband will be receiving plenty of hints that it would make a great anniversary gift."

"I'm glad you like it." The saleswoman reached below the case and retrieved a business card, which she handed to Desi. "Please give him my card. I'll be happy to help him when he comes in here." She winked at Desi. "And maybe I can even get him to buy you a replacement Christmas present."

Desi beamed at her and placed the card in her wallet. "Thank you, I'll be sure to do that."

I murmured my thanks to the woman as well and we pushed the stroller out of the store.

When were out of earshot, we moved to a bench under a shade tree and sat down.

"We didn't learn much about the robbery," I said.

"But we did learn that it was most likely a man," Desi said. "And that necklace was beautiful. If I get it for our anniversary, that will have been time well spent."

We both laughed.

16

*A*fter we returned from town, the guys were still gone, so I left Ella with Desi and took Goldie on a walk. He nosed around down near the lake and I had to hold tight to his leash to keep him from chasing ducks. We ended up on the path along the lakeside.

Goldie saw a squirrel and almost tugged the leash out of my hands.

"Whoa." I stumbled over a tree root as I chased after him. He was getting too close to Tyler's house and I didn't want him near the neighbor's dog, even if it was chained up.

He barked a few times and tugged again. Before I realized it, we were in the clearing in front of Tyler's cabin. I thought about hightailing it out of there, but something made me pause. The saleswoman at the jewelry store had told Desi and me that the robber had been male, but their face had been covered by a black knit face mask, hiding any identifiable facial characteristics.

If Jed had been the robber, would Tyler have known about it? Leah said they were drinking buddies, so there was always the possibility that Jed could have had loose lips and confided in his friend. But did I really expect Tyler to admit to that? Somehow, I had to work my way up to asking him and find out.

I scanned the clearing. I didn't see or hear the dog anywhere—whether that was good or bad, I didn't know. Just in case, I pulled Goldie in close to me, making good use of his canine school training.

From around the corner of the cabin came the sound of chopping wood. I walked toward the sound, and when I could confirm it was Tyler, I shouted, "Hi."

He turned, resting the head of the ax on the ground and wiping sweat off his brow. "Is there something I can do for you? This is private property."

"I wanted to invite you to the Labor Day celebration at the resort this weekend."

"Uh huh. I'm sure Del would love that." He spat into the dirt, leaving a wet spot in the dust.

I averted my eyes and tried to focus on Tyler. "I'm sure he would. I know they're eager to share the resort with the community this weekend."

Also, it wouldn't hurt for Tyler and the resort to make up. I knew firsthand how dreadful it could be to feud with a neighbor.

"Of course he is. There's nothing Del wants more than to be seen as a benefactor in the community."

I cocked my head to the side. "I'm sorry?"

He scoffed. "According to Jed, Del isn't as squeaky clean as he wants people to believe."

I stepped backwards. "What do you mean?"

"Del makes himself out to be better than everyone else, but he's nothing but a criminal himself."

I took that to mean Tyler thought Del considered

himself to be better than him, but I wasn't sure what he meant by calling Del a criminal.

"What are you saying?"

"Why don't you ask him yourself?" He pulled off his ball cap and wiped the sweat off his forehead again. "Jed knew some things about his cousin that Del didn't want made known to everyone else."

My head was reeling. I'd always thought of Del as a nice guy, admittedly, just as Tyler had implied the community thought of him. But talking about Del wasn't why I'd ventured onto Tyler's property.

"Did Jed tell you he wanted to go into business with Del back home?"

Tyler laughed. "He had some far-fetched idea about opening a bar. Wasn't ever going to happen. Jed was grasping at straws if he ever thought he'd see a dime of that money."

"Do you know where the money came from?"

"Nah, it was from somebody he'd done business with in the past. But he'd been bragging about it for a while and it never materialized."

"So it wasn't a more recent idea of his?"

He shook his head. "No. Why are you so interested in Jed's money anyway?"

"Not really any reason. Del had mentioned it and I was just curious."

From the other side of the shiny silver pickup truck, a dog started barking.

"Duke, shut it!" Tyler yelled. The dog ran toward us, and I prepared to flee with Goldie. Duke stopped next to his owner, barking furiously at us. Tyler grabbed his collar as I backed away slowly.

"Uh, well, remember, you're welcome at the celebration this weekend."

Tyler didn't say a word.

Goldie stayed close to my side as we made it to the trail and then ran back to the resort as fast as we could. When we reached the resort property line, I looked behind us, terrified that Tyler would have let Duke loose to chase us. Luckily, the trail was empty.

I sat down to catch my breath, Goldie milling around next to me, not worrying about a thing. I wished I could forget traumatic events that quickly. A lawnmower roared, and I spotted Del on the riding lawnmower, mowing the grass near the lake.

I shivered, despite the warm weather. I'd always thought of Del as a nice guy, but Tyler had made me wonder what was hidden in Del's past. Was it something so bad that Del could have killed to keep it a secret? And if there really was money from a past business venture, did that mean he hadn't robbed the jewelry store? Although I didn't want to think ill of Del's cousin, the thought was deflating. I'd talked myself into thinking Jed was a jewelry store robber and now I worried I might have missed another piece of the puzzle while focusing on that thread.

"What does everyone want to do today?" Tomàs asked, sipping his coffee on their deck.

I leaned back in my chair. All I really wanted to do was to laze around near our cabin, but I didn't think that was the answer he was looking for.

"We could hang out around here; maybe take the kids to the playground for an hour or so?" Desi rocked Lina in her arms. "Tomorrow will be pretty exciting with the celebration. I know I could use a relaxing day doing nothing."

I hid a grin. I wasn't surprised that Desi didn't want to do anything exerting. Being a mom on a "vacation" with kids was exhausting enough.

"I was thinking we could go out on the lake? Either in rowboats or a canoe?" Adam suggested.

Tomàs nodded. "Sounds fun. I wanted to get some canoeing in."

Desi and I looked at each other and I shrugged.

"Do they have life jackets that will fit Lina?" Desi asked.

"I don't know." Tomàs jangled their cabin keys. "Let's find out."

The boys bounded out the door, followed by our husbands, and Desi and I brought up the rear with the babies.

Tomàs led us to the boathouse where the life jackets were kept. I held my breath as we neared the door. Since half of the life jackets had been burned, I didn't know if we'd find the sizes we needed. With any luck there wouldn't be enough for Desi, me, and the babies.

He flung open the door and disappeared inside. "Woohoo! We're in luck."

Behind me, Desi sighed. Tomàs came out carrying an armful of life jackets which he distributed to us.

"I hope we can get a boat. There are fewer life jackets here than I'd expect."

I focused on fastening the straps on my flotation device, then put Ella's on her while Adam did the same with his and Mikey's.

Our last chance of getting out of canoeing was for there not to be enough boats. Unfortunately, there were two double canoes left and a paddleboat.

"How about we take the canoes and you and Jill take the paddleboat. That way you can hold the babies while still paddling," Tomàs said to Desi.

"Sounds good."

He helped us into the paddleboat and pushed us away from the dock. When we were safely out on the lake, he said, "Last ones out on the lake are rotten eggs!"

The boys giggled and clambered into the boats as their dads held the watercraft steady.

"Ha! We win!" Adam shouted, triumphantly pumping his paddle in the air.

Tomàs pointed to a spot further down the lake. "Race you to that stand of trees."

"You're on." Adam dipped his paddle into the lake and urged Mikey to do the same.

"We'd better get out of the way of these macho men." Desi peddled to turn us and we moved about twenty feet out of the path of the canoes.

They slid past us in haphazard patterns as the dads tried to compensate for the little boys' weaker paddling.

"I feel like the whole racing thing was a bad idea." Desi stared at them as we floated lazily on the lake.

"Probably. Luckily, it's not our problem. The guys can figure it out."

"Want to go back in?" Desi asked, her eyes dancing. "I don't think they'll miss us."

I smiled. "We can claim Lina needed to be fed."

"Good plan." She started peddling and I joined in.

Soon, we were back at the docks. By this time, the two canoes were tiny specks on the other side of the lake.

Ten minutes later, we were relaxing on the deck of Adam's and my cabin.

"Ah," Desi said. "Now this is nice."

The babies had fallen asleep immediately when we got back to the cabins and we'd made a fresh pot of coffee to take out to the deck.

"Yeah. It's amazing how quiet it is without all the guys." I closed my eyes, enjoying the warmth out on the screened-in deck.

I was almost asleep when a knock sounded on the door.

I walked back inside the cabin and opened it.

"Hey," I said. "What's up?"

Tears filled Leah's eyes. "Are you busy? I was hoping you might have time to talk. I could use a friend right now."

"Nope, Desi and I were just hanging out on the deck. All of our menfolk are out showing their racing prowess on the lake." I laughed and motioned for her to come inside. "You're welcome to join us."

She jutted her chin toward the deck. "You're sure Desi won't mind?"

"Nope," Desi said, ducking her head inside the cabin. "C'mon. I'm thinking about switching to wine soon."

"Isn't it too early?" Leah glanced at the brass clock on the wall.

Desi shrugged. "It's almost eleven and we're on vacation. Besides, I think we've only got about an hour before the babies wake up and the boys come back. Might as well enjoy ourselves while we can."

Leah laughed. "Ok, count me in. I'll take a glass of something."

"Coming right up." Desi moved across the cabin, toward the kitchen.

I touched Leah's arm. "We're outside. Come sit."

She followed me out there and Desi returned with three glasses of wine.

"Thanks." Leah took the glass and sat back in her chair.

"So what's up? You look a little down." I sipped my wine but kept my eyes on her.

"It's a little of everything. More cancellations, the vandalism, everything." She ran her finger over the rim of the glass, making it sing. "And I don't have Del to lean on anymore." Her eyes filled with fresh tears.

"I'm so sorry, Leah." I went over to her and hugged her. "I'm sure this isn't what you signed up for."

"No." She sobbed. "The resort was a dream of both Del and I, but now it's just me."

"Do you think it might be time to sell?" Desi asked. "I know it's tough to let go, but sometimes when something is making you miserable it's better to move on."

Leah hung her head. "I know. And it is making miserable—right now." She looked up at us. "But what if it gets better? We've had so many good times here."

"I don't know what to tell you," I said. "You have to make that decision on your own. But with everything going on this week, I don't think this is the best time to do so."

She nodded. "You're probably right. I just wish I had a clearer idea of what I should do. I do know that I don't want to go back to working in the city." She gestured widely. "After being out here in such beautiful nature, I can't return to a concrete jungle."

"Well, I think that gives you part of your answer—what you don't want," Desi said. "Maybe that will help you make your decision."

"Maybe."

We were quiet for a few minutes, gazing out at the peaceful lake.

"Hey, isn't that Tomàs and Adam?" Desi pointed to two canoes darting across the lake.

I squinted. "I think so."

Ten minutes later, we had our answer, in the form of the loud approach of two excited four-year-olds.

"Daddy and I won the first race," Anthony bragged.

Mikey glared at his cousin. "But my daddy and I beat you home."

"Did not," Anthony said.

"Did too." Mikey stuck out his tongue.

Desi and I exchanged glances.

"Where are your daddies?" Desi asked.

Mikey pointed behind him. "They're coming. We ran up from the docks."

"I have to go potty, so they let us go ahead." Anthony danced from foot to foot.

Desi sighed and pointed at the bathroom. "Go now!"

"Do I have to go right now?" He stared longingly at the Hungry Hungry Hippos box on an end table.

"Yes!" Desi shooed him off.

Leah grinned at the kids' antics. "I'm going to get back to work now. Thanks for the talk, girls. I really appreciated it and I feel a little better now."

"Good," I said, giving her a quick hug out on the small porch. "That's what we're here for."

"If I don't see you again today, I hope you have a wonderful afternoon." She glanced up. "This weather is just perfect." She waved and trotted off in the direction of the office.

Tomàs and Adam arrived a few minutes later.

"The boys beat you back," I said.

"Yeah, well, they weren't expending much energy paddling." Adam's face was flushed.

"Did you have a good time?" Desi asked sweetly.

"We did." Tomàs eyed Adam. "We raced each other a few times, and were going for the tiebreaker, but then

Anthony had to use the bathroom, so we decided to head in."

"Now we're going to have to find something else to break the tie." Adam looked around, but evidently didn't find anything appropriate for competition.

I groaned inwardly. *Great.* I'd wanted them to bond, but I hadn't anticipated them to both have a competitive streak. In hindsight, I should have known from their performances at family game nights.

"I'm sure you'll find something tomorrow," I said. "For now, we should figure out what we're having for lunch."

"Ok, ok," said Adam.

We spent the afternoon outside on the green grass, eating turkey and cheese sandwiches with pickles and potato chips. We'd borrowed a game of lawn darts from the office and somehow Desi and I were able to keep our husbands from making it into an intense competition. Later, we all took naps, then went to the café for dinner. It was exactly the lazy kind of day I'd envisioned for our trip.

I'd promised the boys that I'd take them to get ice cream treats at the office/general store, so after dinner we trekked along the dusty road to get there. When we arrived, there was no one there. Someone had stuck a card on the front counter. *Be back in ten minutes.*

I let Mikey and Anthony rifle through the chest freezer in search of the perfect novelty ice cream.

"Rainbow sherbet?" Anthony asked, holding up a push-pop.

"Or chocolate? Or an ice cream sandwich?" Mikey said with his head deep in the freezer. He was leaning so far in that his feet didn't quite touch the ground. I grabbed the waistband of his jeans and eased him out of there.

"Did you decide yet?"

"No," Anthony said sheepishly. "There's too many choices."

I smiled. I'd been there myself as a child. Who was I kidding? I still had trouble choosing ice cream at the store. One day at the grocery store when I was pregnant with Ella, I found myself debating between two flavors of ice cream for thirty minutes before deciding to buy both of them.

"How about you choose three, then pick a number and I'll tell you which one that is? We can get more ice cream tomorrow, I promise."

The boys looked at each other. "Ok," they said in unison.

"I choose one hundred and eighty," Mikey shouted, jumping up and down.

"Uh ..." I may have needed to be more specific. "How about you choose one of these numbers—one, two, or three."

"Three!" Anthony said, his eyes sparkling with excitement.

"I want number three too. Which one is that?" Mikey scanned the selection.

"You've won orange sherbet and vanilla ice cream popsicles!" I waved two of them at the kids with a flourish, and the ice cream treats were immediately torn from my grip.

I selected an ice cream cookie sandwich for myself. I was on vacation and walking over to Tyler's cabin with Goldie counted as exercise, right? After all, there had been running involved.

There still wasn't anyone at the counter, so I grabbed a sticky note from behind the counter and left a note with five dollars under it on top of the cash register. I wouldn't normally do that, but Leah was a friend and I knew she wouldn't mind. Besides, if I didn't get the kids out of the store soon, their ice cream would melt all over the linoleum floors.

We went outside and sat on the bench next to the hanging flower baskets to eat our treats. The boys licked their popsicles, happily swinging their legs under the bench. A small box truck bearing the name of the general store in town rumbled up the dirt road, bouncing over the potholes, then pulled up to the office in front of us.

The driver kept the engine running for a few minutes while he did something with a clipboard in the front seat, filling the area with diesel fumes. Anthony and Mikey coughed.

I motioned for them to get up. "Let's go over to the playground, boys." They slowly complied, but we had to wait for Mikey when his ice cream wrapper flew away and he chased after it.

The driver finally turned off the engine and walked into the office. The air cleared and I could breathe more normally, but Mikey was taking a long time.

"C'mon," I said.

He stuck his head under another bench. "It went under here." He bent down then wriggled under it.

The truck driver came out. "Ma'am, do you know if there is someone here at the store? There doesn't seem to be anyone and I've got merchandise to unload."

I craned my head around to see if Del or Leah were anywhere nearby. "I'm sorry, I really don't know. What's in the truck?"

"A few dozen life jackets. The customers put a rush order on them, so I really need to deliver them today. But I can't just leave them here."

I nodded. "Maybe I can help. I'm a friend of the owners."

"Could you possibly sign for them?" He held out the clipboard I'd seen him writing on in the truck cab.

I checked for Del and Leah again. Still no sign of them. I knew they needed the life jackets as soon as possible though and I didn't think they'd mind if I accepted the delivery.

"Sure. I think that would be fine." I reached out for the clipboard.

"Seems like a lot of life jackets to order this late in the season," the driver observed. "We usually get orders in April or May for new ones."

"Yeah, well, I think they wanted to have everything nice and new for the Labor Day celebration out here tomorrow." It wasn't exactly the truth, but it wasn't a lie either. They did want things to be nice for the event.

The bright sun made it difficult to see the words on the clipboard, so I shielded my eyes with my hand and squinted at the information on the document. "Where do I sign?"

He stabbed a stubby finger at a line near the bottom of the piece of paper. "Right here."

I caught sight of the total and gasped. Over a thousand dollars for life jackets. Leah hadn't been kidding about the financial toll of the escalating vandalism.

I set the pen down on the clipboard without signing. "I don't think I should sign for this much money."

The delivery driver didn't look happy, but he simply said "ok." He looked around. "Do you think we might be able to find the owners so I can get these out of my truck?"

I nodded and turned to the boys. "Mikey, Anthony, we have to go."

Mikey emerged from under the bench and tossed the plastic wrapper in the trash, along with the wooden stick for his ice cream. Anthony finished chewing on his almost bare stick and threw his in there as well. They followed dutifully behind the delivery driver and me as we walked further into the resort, heading toward Leah's house. Out of the corner of my eye, I saw Desi strolling across the grassy lawn.

"Hey," I greeted her. "Can you watch the boys while I help this man find Leah or Del? He's got a delivery that needs a signature."

"Yeah, no problem." She called out to the kids, "Come over to me, please." They came closer and she leaned down to talk to them. "You can play on the playground for a while, but then I need to get you ready for bed."

The boys shouted with joy and immediately raced over to the playground.

The delivery driver and I walked away, passing the campfire pit above our cabin. He lingered near it, ogling the area surrounding the fire pit.

"Is that where they found the dead guy? I heard he had a marshmallow roasting stick lodged in his back. Is that true?"

I sighed. I understood his curiosity, but I didn't want to think about Jed's body lying next to the fire pit. "Yes. He was found right over there." I pointed at the dirt next to the small cabinet where the s'mores equipment was kept.

His eyes widened. "Wow. I can't believe that happened here. We've had more crime in the area this week than I've heard of in all my life."

"Yeah, we got here the day of the jewelry store robbery. It seemed like that was a pretty big talk of the town."

He shook his head up and down rapidly. "Nothing like that has ever happened before. I mean, I work for the general store, and sometimes we get, you know, kids stealing a candy bar or something once in a while, but stealing hundreds of thousands of dollars' worth of diamonds? That's unheard of."

"Who do you think could have stolen the diamonds?" I asked, as we hiked up the hill toward Leah's house.

"I don't know, but rumor is that Mr. Junell had been shooting off his mouth in the bar about his design job and the delivery of the diamonds, so it could've been anybody who was in there with him."

"Hmm. That's so crazy."

He looked down, over the lake. "I haven't been out here much, but I also make deliveries for the hardware store and one time I delivered a load of wood to the guy that lives over there." He motioned to Tyler's cabin.

"Oh, really?" I scanned the area, hoping Del would magically show up.

"Yeah. He's a carpenter or something and someone had ordered custom cabinets from him, but there was a flaw in the wood he picked up at the lumber yard, so they had me bring him a replacement." He shuddered. "That dog of his kept barking at me the whole time I was there. I never took my eye off it until I was safely back in the cab."

I nodded. "I know what you mean. I've seen that dog and I wouldn't want to be alone with it, that's for sure." We reached Leah's house and I knocked on the door.

"Coming!"

She came to the door with her hair up in a towel turban.

"Hi." She looked behind me to the delivery man. "Is there a problem?"

"Nope, he's just here to deliver the new life jackets. I didn't feel comfortable signing for them."

She tilted her head to the side. "Where was Del?"

"I'm not sure. There was a note on the counter saying someone would be back soon, but no one was there."

"I left a message for him that it was his turn in the office, but maybe he didn't get it." She held up one finger. "Give me a minute and I'll come check out the delivery and sign for it."

We waited on her front steps while she ran inside to finish dressing. When she came out, she'd wound her wet hair up in a bun and changed into jeans and a tank top.

"Do you mind if I head back to our cabin?" I asked.

"No, thanks so much for helping. I can't believe Del didn't show up for work. I'll see you later." She and the delivery driver left and I walked back to the cabin.

On the way back, I saw Del out on the docks, and I briefly considered mentioning to him that Leah thought he would be at the office, but I decided to stay out of it. My meddling didn't always turn out well and things were messy enough between them as is.

17

*L*abor Day arrived and I woke up excited for the day's festivities, but sad that we'd be heading home the next day. Our vacation at Thunder Lake Resort hadn't been exactly what I expected, but I'd enjoyed our time there nonetheless. Next to me in bed, Adam was still asleep. I tiptoed over to the window in our room, lifted the curtains and peeked out the window. The sky was blue and the sun was already shining brightly.

A smile stretched across my lips and I sighed in happiness. Today was going to be a good day. Although we were technically on vacation, I'd loved getting to help Leah with her event. I actually missed going in to work every day at the Boathouse. Well, except for dealing with clients like Angela Laveaux. This event was even more important than most as it meant so much to Leah. I hated seeing her so stressed-out. I knew she enjoyed owning the resort, but I had to wonder if Del was right to worry about her being so wrapped up in it.

"Honey," Adam said groggily. "What time is it?"

"I think it's around seven a.m." I glanced at my watch. "Yep. Seven fifteen."

"Do I need to get up yet? It seems really early on the last day of our vacation."

"Nope, I just couldn't sleep." I pointed at the main living area in the cabin. "I'm going to go check on the kids and start a pot of coffee, ok?"

"Works for me. Let me know if you need me to get up and help with anything." His head crashed back down to the pillow.

Goldie followed me out and I quietly shut the bedroom door behind us then went over to the bedroom where the kids were sleeping. They were both still out. I closed their door, started a pot of coffee, and plopped down on the couch. Perfect. We'd left some windows cracked last night and the air inside the cabin was fresh. Sun shone in, creating glowing yellow patches on the floor.

The coffee finished percolating and I grabbed a cup then went outside with Goldie to sit on the porch. It was even more peaceful out here. A few people were already out fishing on the still lake, but there was no sound from the rest of the resort. The only thing breaking the quiet was Goldie softly thumping the floor with his tail as he watched the birds in the trees adjacent to our covered deck.

I got about thirty minutes of alone time in before Ella started stirring. I picked her up out of the Pack 'n Play and dressed her for the day. Her crying had woken Mikey up, and the three of us went out to the living room for an easy meal of Cheerios with milk.

Adam rose from bed and hopped into the shower, then came out to relieve me so I could do the same. When I emerged from the bathroom they were all out on the lawn playing catch with Goldie.

"What's on the agenda for today? What time does the Labor Day celebration start?" Adam removed the small ball from Goldie's mouth and tossed it to Mikey, who then threw it in the general direction of the dog.

"The egg toss, three-legged race, and tug-of-war are the first things. Then the barbecue lunch." I leaned against the cabin to watch them. "The boat races start after we eat."

"Are we participating in any of them?"

"I hadn't planned on it, but you're welcome to if you want. I've got to manage them and I'm charged with coordinating the ribbons at the end of each event."

"So, no egg toss for you?" Adam teased me. "Your mom once told me how much you *loved* egg tosses. Said you'd had a great time at one when you were little."

I gave him a dirty look. "Haha." I shuddered. When I was a kid, I'd participated in an egg toss that had left my hair dripping with egg yolks and whites. My mother had tried to convince me that it was good conditioning for my hair, but I could still remember the slime dripping down into my ears. I'd had a fear of egg tosses ever since that day.

"Well, maybe Mikey and I will participate in the three-legged race." He looked over at Mikey. "Does that sound like fun?"

Mikey cocked his head to the side. "What is that?"

Adam pressed his leg up against Mikey's. "We tie our legs together like this and then have to move our legs at the same time. See—three legs."

"Cool! Yeah, we're going to win because I'm really good at moving my legs like that."

I smothered a grin as Adam fought to do the same, unsuccessfully.

"Sounds like a plan. Now, does anyone want to go play on the playground?" I asked Mikey.

"Is Anthony up?"

"I don't know, let's go see." We walked over to the

Torres's cabin. They were all sitting out on their porch having scrambled eggs.

"Hey, guys." Desi held out a spatula and a frying pan. "Do you want some? I didn't want to take any of the eggs home with us, so I made them all." She frowned. "We'll be eating eggs for dinner if you don't help us out."

"Sure. I didn't eat yet." Adam followed her into the cabin and came out with a full plate.

I took the boys over to the playground for an hour, then dropped them off with Desi so I could work on the event coordination. Happily, everything seemed ready to go. Del and Leah were preparing for the boat race and setup for the catering crew, and I was in charge of the morning's games. They'd given me permission to have the resort staff help get the games ready, but everybody seemed busy.

Sela walked by, not carrying anything, and I stopped her.

"Hey, can you please help me fill the mud pit for the tug-of-war? I'm not sure where the hose is and I have to run back to my cabin and get the ribbons and medals for the events." I laughed. "There will be a revolt if I'm not there, ready with the prizes for the winners."

She eyed me disdainfully. "Can't. I've got stuff to do." Without another word, she strode off. I rolled my eyes and got back to work. Luckily, Del came by and filled the mud pit for me with a hose he pulled out of the storage shed.

People trickled down to the grassy lawn next to the lake from their cabins and drove in from town. A fire truck and police car had been decorated and stationed near the office for kids to climb in and take pictures with. I set up the egg toss and got out of the way so I wouldn't get hit by a stray egg. After I handed the winners and the participants their ribbons for that event, I put out the stretchy bands that would be used to tie the "third leg" together in the three-legged race.

Mikey and Anthony ran up, with their fathers in tow. Desi followed with the babies in the double stroller.

"We're going to win. My daddy is faster than yours," Anthony boasted.

Mikey stuck his tongue out at his cousin. "No, we're going to win, right, Daddy?" He looked up at Adam.

"I think we'll have to see who's the fastest," Adam said diplomatically.

All of the contestants lined up. At the end, two other father-and-son teams loudly jostled for position. I eyed them. I'd seen them around the resort, most recently in the recreation hall. The pre-teen boys had been fighting over whose turn it was to play the solitary arcade game in the hall. Were they going to be trouble now?

Unfortunately, the answer to my question was yes. Halfway down the grass course, they veered toward each other, all four of them toppling to the ground. The fathers started yelling at each other and the kids were wrestling next to them. As they got louder and louder, everyone else stopped what they were doing to watch the commotion.

Tomàs jogged over to the brawlers. "Hey, hey, break it up. This is a family event."

I was glad he'd stepped in. As a police officer, he was trained in conflict resolution and I'd seen him diffuse such situations before.

"Back off," one of the men said. "This guy has had it out for me since we accidentally cut him off out on the lake a few days ago."

"You did it on purpose." The other man glared at his foe.

Before the first man could form a retort, Tomàs had skillfully maneuvered him away from the situation. Adam plucked the bigger boy off of the other, holding him back from hurting the other kid.

"Let's all calm down here." Tomàs looked from one man to the other. "There are kids here. I don't think you want anyone to get hurt, right?"

"No," they both grumbled, their eyes still shooting daggers at one another. They each grabbed their kids and stalked off from the grassy lawn.

I breathed a sigh of relief. Sometimes having a brother-in-law who was a police officer could come in handy.

"Thanks, Tomàs." I clapped my hands and addressed the rest of contestants, who were gathered nearby, watching the spectacle. "Now, since we all got distracted, let's start over, ok? Everyone back to the starting line."

They started over, and this time a team made it to the finish line.

"Aww. We didn't win," said Mikey.

"Us neither," Anthony said glumly.

I handed the first place ribbon to the winners, a mother and her daughter who looked to be about seven. Everyone clapped and the little girl jumped up and down in excitement. She bounced off with her mother and the crowd dispersed.

"Well, I think that was enough excitement for the day," I said to Adam.

He nodded. "Some people take these competitions way too seriously."

"So you're not going to participate in the tug-of-war?"

He gave me a wounded look. "Of course I'm going to help with the tug-of-war. I've got to beat Tomàs at something."

I laughed. "May the stronger team win."

Desi, the kids, and I watched from the sidelines as

Tomàs and Adam, on opposite sides, fought to drag their opponents into the mud pit in the center. As Adam's team slid closer to the pit, I walked closer, ready to call a winner. The team Tomàs was on gave a final tug and the game was over.

Adam had been near the back of the line, and he walked away with only a few splashes of mud on his legs and shoes. Those that were near the front were not so lucky. I stifled a laugh when a man walked past me covered in oozing mud. He didn't seem to mind and, in fact, was racing down to the lake with his kids to jump in and wash off.

The aroma of fresh barbecue wafted over to us. I'd handed day-of responsibility for the catering over to Leah so I could focus on the games, but I was curious to see how the food would taste. My event duties were over for the morning and my stomach was grumbling. I regretted not taking some of the eggs Desi had offered. Under a large canopy tent set up next to the picnic tables, the caterers appeared to be ready to serve.

"Lunchtime!" I announced.

Adam eyed Tomàs. "Race you to the lunch line."

"You're on," Tomàs replied.

They both took off, leaving us staring at them.

"Seriously?" Desi asked. "What is with the competition between them now?"

I shrugged. "Give them one thing to compete over, and it's suddenly a tournament."

"Maybe we tell them we're giving out a 'best dad' award and watch them fall over themselves trying to best each other in taking care of the kids."

I shook my finger at her. "You may be on to something there. If I have any leftover ribbons, I'll keep one and we can try it."

We both laughed and guided the kids over to the lunch area. Tomàs and Adam were already there, holding plates of food. I didn't know who had won the race, and I wasn't going to ask.

I looked around. Everything was going according to plan, an event planner's dream. We were all finishing up our lunch of barbecue pork, corn on the cob, coleslaw, and corn-bread that the restaurant in town had catered. All around us, people wore satisfied expressions as they mopped barbecue sauce off of their faces.

"When are the boats going to race?" Mikey asked, scanning the lake for any sign of action.

Below the gently sloping lawn, paddle-powered boats had been decorated with flags and a number. They floated by the docks, ready for their contestants to jump aboard.

I checked my watch. Almost one o'clock. Del was in charge of the boat races and he was on the docks, checking things out. I had the gold medal for the winner, but I was free from event duties until then.

"Soon, Mikey."

Almost one o'clock also meant that Goldie had been left in our cabin for several hours already. I didn't think he'd get in any trouble, but I wanted to take him out for a walk to make sure.

"Can you take the kids down to the lakeshore to get a good viewpoint for the races?" I asked. "I'm going to go check on Goldie."

"Yep." Adam glanced at Mikey's mouth, which had brown sauce dripping from it like a barbecue zombie. "After I get this kid hosed down."

I laughed. "I don't care how you do it, but get the sauce off before he gets it all over everything. And don't forget to keep Ella's hat on, ok?"

He saluted me. "Aye, aye, captain."

"Hey, I'm not racing today," I joked. I rose from the picnic table and brushed some cornbread crumbs off my lap. "I'll see you in thirty minutes or so."

"We'll save you a seat," he said absentmindedly as he scrubbed at Mikey's face with a water-dampened paper towel.

Desi popped up too. "I'll tag along. I want to grab some more sunscreen from our cabin."

"Sure." We walked back toward our cabins, away from the crowds.

She branched off at the fork in the path and went into her cabin, while I approached ours. I stopped. Something wasn't right. It was strangely quiet for housing a friendly dog who'd be awaiting his family's arrival. I quickened my pace as I rounded the corner to the front door. The screen was open.

"Goldie?" I called out as I ran into the cabin. If he'd managed to push the door open, I didn't think he would go far, but this was unfamiliar territory and the prospect of catching a squirrel could entice even the most obedient dog into a long chase.

I hurriedly searched every room in the cabin, but Goldie wasn't there. I eyed the door. I could have sworn we'd locked it. Goldie was smart, but not smart enough to unlock a door and open it.

A chill traveled through my body. Was this some kind of joke? It didn't look like anything had been stolen from our cabin. Adam's tablet was on the table and my purse was where I'd left it on an end table in our bedroom. So why was Goldie gone?

A piece of yellow paper taped to the wall next to the

door caught my eye. That hadn't been there earlier. I walked over to it and plucked it off the wall.

Your dog is taking a little vacation. You might want to come get him before he's eaten by the neighbor's dog.

The blood drained from my face. Someone was threatening Goldie's life. Was it the same person who was vandalizing the resort?

Footsteps crunched along the pathway outside of our cabin, and I craned my neck around to see who it was. Only Desi. I moved my attention back to the note.

"Are you ready to head back? I had to scrounge around for it, but I finally found some sunscreen in the medicine cabinet. Tomàs always insists on unpacking every time we stay somewhere, but then I can't find anything. I knew where everything was when it was in the suitcases." She stopped and I felt her eyes on me. "What's wrong? What is that you're looking at?" She came around behind me and read over my shoulder.

I let her grab it out of my trembling hands.

"Someone stole Goldie? Who would do that?"

"I don't know. But I think he's over at Tyler's house."

"That creepy guy with the dog with the big teeth?" Her eyes widened.

"Yeah." I glanced in the direction of Tyler's place.

"What are you going to do?"

"I'm going to get my dog back." I dropped the note on the floor and stalked off.

Desi jogged along behind me. "You can't go by yourself. Let's go get Adam and Tomàs."

I turned my head slightly. "That would take at least another fifteen minutes. Who knows how long Goldie's been gone for?"

"Argh," she cried out. "Fine, I'll go with you. You're not

doing this alone." She caught up with me, and we half-ran, half-jogged along the lakeside path, the crowd roaring behind us as the starting pistol went off for the boat races.

At Tyler's house, it was blessedly silent. No sign of him or his dog. I heard a whimper coming from the barn. Goldie.

I threw the doors open, and Desi and I rushed in. When our eyes adjusted, we both looked around frantically for Goldie.

I'd expected the barn's interior to be dusty and coated with hay, or at the very least, full of junk. Instead, the walls were lined with heavy-duty shelves and countertops, along with a wide selection of wood-working tools.

A worktable in the middle of the room held a hand-crafted frame of an armchair, with beautiful scrollwork on it.

Desi ran a finger over a sculpted flower on the back of the chair. "Did that guy do this?"

"I don't know. The delivery man from the general store did say Tyler was a woodworker." I searched the inside of the barn. "But let's focus on finding Goldie right now."

"Right," she said.

We heard another whimper and I slowly spun around.

"Up there." Desi pointed to the hay loft.

"Goldie?"

Scuffling noises followed, along with more whimpers.

"Why isn't he barking?" she asked.

"I don't know." My legs wobbled like they were made of gelatin. What had they done to my dog? "I don't see a ladder."

The floor was bare in a spot where a ladder had recently rested.

"Maybe we could use that rope to get up there?" Desi pointed to a thin rope hanging from the ceiling near the loft.

I shook my head. "There's no way I can climb that. Besides, it's frayed at the top. You look around in here. I'm going to go outside and see what else I can find. We've got to get him down from there."

I exited the front door then navigated around the exterior of the building. Car parts were strewn everywhere, along with empty beer bottles and paint cans. At the back of the barn, there was an open window into the loft. Underneath it, an old truck had been parked alongside the barn, its front end covered by an equally old blue tarp.

"Desi," I shouted. "Come here."

"Where are you?"

"Around the back."

Desi appeared in a matter of seconds. "What?"

I pointed at the cab of the truck. "I think if we climb up there, we can get into the loft through that window."

She eyed the window dubiously. "How are we going to get him out afterwards?"

"I don't know. Right now, all I want to do is find out if he's ok."

I pulled myself up into the bed of the truck and then held my hand out to her to give her a lift.

"Do you think you can brace my feet while I climb in?"

"I can try."

Below our feet, the truck creaked under our weight on the cab.

"I don't know about this." Desi stared at the ground. "I hope it can hold us."

I wondered the same thing, but at this point, we didn't have a choice. I didn't know where the dognapper was or when they were coming back. So far, the acts of vandalism hadn't been violent, but I didn't want to take any chances. At the back of my mind, a little voice reminded me that Jed's murderer hadn't been found. What if the vandal and the murderer were the same person? I shook the thought from my head. Right now, I needed to focus on Goldie.

"Can you give me a boost?" I moved as close to the edge of the truck cab as I could and leaned against the barn. Even with my arms outstretched, the window was at least a foot above me.

Desi threaded her hands together and I stepped on the makeshift stirrup, giving me enough of a boost to pop my chin over the edge. Goldie lay on a blanket on the floor of the loft, chained to a beam with his mouth muzzled. Tears sprang from my eyes, wetting my cheeks.

"He's here and he looks ok," I shouted down to Desi. "Can you lift me up a little?"

She responded by raising her arms, allowing me enough leverage to get through the window. Although I wasn't super fit, I had some arm strength from lugging around two small children on a daily basis.

I fell onto the wooden loft floor in an undignified heap, and Goldie strained to get closer to me.

"It's ok, boy." I crawled toward him, holding out my hand. "I'll get you free." I removed the muzzle and he licked me. As I was figuring out how to release the chain from his collar, he started barking ferociously and tried to get to the edge of the loft that overlooked the main room of the barn.

I looked over the edge to see who'd entered. I hoped it wasn't Tyler and his dog.

It wasn't Tyler.

"Sela?"

Her head shot up to view me and her eyes widened.

"How did you get up there? I took the ladder and stashed it in the woods."

I ignored her question as I didn't want to put Desi in danger. "Why did you take Goldie?"

She laughed. "When you aren't there, the whole celebration will fall apart. It'll be pretty embarrassing when you're not there to hand out the medal for the big boat race. Then they'll have to sell the resort and Del will be free of Leah."

I stared at her. She was crazier than I'd thought. "You put my dog in danger for that? Were you behind all the other acts of vandalism?"

"I can't confirm that," she said smugly. "But let's just say that other than you being here, my plan is going quite well. And if you try to say I put your dog up there, I'll deny it. It's your word against mine."

"Did you kill Jed?"

"What? Why would you think that?" She shot me a wounded look. "I may have wanted the resort to fail, but what reason would I have to kill Del's cousin? He was devastated by Jed's death."

"So you didn't kill him?"

"No, of course not." She looked miffed. "I was visiting my family in Spokane the day he was killed. You can call them and confirm."

I'd hoped the murderer had been caught, but unfortunately, I thought she was telling me the truth.

She saw the thin rope hanging next to the loft. "Ah, that's how you got up there." She pulled on the end of it, looping it over the edge of a hook on the wall. "That should keep you away for a while longer."

She waved at me, grinning maniacally. "See you later."

When she was gone, Desi appeared in the barn. "I heard what Sela said—she's even battier than we thought." She stared up at me. "Now, how are we going to get you and Goldie down from there?"

I pointed at the rope. The frayed fibers were even more evident from this height. "I think if you pull on that hard enough, it will break at the top. It's barely hanging on by a thread."

She yanked on it, and it tumbled down, spiraling in the air like a snake as it fell. "Now what?"

"I can probably tie it onto something up here to get down, but let's get Goldie down first." I released the chain from his collar. "He's a smart dog, but I don't think he can climb down a rope. We've got to find something to use as a harness lift."

She snapped her fingers. "The tarp outside, on the hood of the truck. We can loop the rope through the holes in it and make a sack for Goldie."

"Good idea." Goldie and I walked over to the window, peering down as Desi maneuvered the tarp off the truck.

I lowered the rope down and Desi wove it through the holes, then through the loose end of the rope up to me. I caught it and pulled up the harness. I placed Goldie in the tarp and put the whole thing on the wide window ledge. He whimpered.

"It's ok, boy." I patted his head. "Stay."

I wrapped the rope around a post and tied the other end around my waist before gently pushing the bundle over the edge. I made a mental note to thank my dad for the hours he'd spent teaching me knot-tying techniques when I was a kid. The rope slid along the post, then caught as my body weight slowed Goldie's descent before Desi could help guide him down. Then, I pulled it back up, tied the rope to the beam, and rappelled down the side.

Desi's eyes widened. "Wow, I didn't know you knew how to do that."

"Adam and I took rock climbing lessons before the kids were born."

"Ah. One of those things that childless people get to do on dates."

"Yep." Still on the cab of the truck, I leaned down to hug Goldie, who was wriggling around. He returned the gesture of love by licking my face. "Well I'm ready to get out of here."

Desi didn't hear me—the front of the truck had drawn her attention. "Uh, Jill?"

"What?" I followed her gaze. The truck's front end had been smashed in so much that I wondered how Tyler had driven it back here.

"Didn't the saleswoman at the jewelry store say that the robber smashed down the back wall with a truck?" She pointed at the damage. "That could certainly be the result of running into a concrete block wall."

A sinking feeling hit my stomach. "Do you remember what she said about the back workroom being recently remodeled?"

"Tyler's a carpenter."

"Uh huh."

We both stared at the barn. I didn't know why we hadn't put it together sooner. Tyler and Jed had been friends, so it made sense that if Jed had robbed the store, Tyler might have been his accomplice. And if Tyler knew Jed had the diamonds ...

"Desi, we've got to get out of here."

Her face turned white and she nodded.

We scrambled down onto the truck bed, Goldie jumping down next to us.

"What are you doing here?" Tyler's voice was unyielding.

18

I inadvertently looked at the front of the truck.

"Yeah, I heard you and your friend talking," Tyler said.

Desi's eyes bugged out and my stomach lurched. Goldie barked loudly.

"Keep your dog quiet," Tyler ordered.

I held Goldie close to calm him down and we tried to edge our way back in the truck bed.

He regarded us with shrewd eyes, as if deciding what to do about us.

I pointed to the newer truck parked near the house. Tyler's dog had jumped into the back, and I could see suitcases stacked inside the truck bed.

"It looks like you're going somewhere. Just let us go. We won't say anything until you're far out of town."

He grinned at us. "No, you're not going to say anything—because you won't be alive to do so."

He pulled a gun on us and ordered us down from the truck, then herded us toward the front of the barn.

"Why did you kill Jed? To get the diamonds?"

"Of course. I had to kill him. That idiot wouldn't have lasted a week with them before telling someone about the robbery. But then I couldn't find his share of the diamonds. Got them now though. He'd hidden them in an Arizona Diamondbacks ball cap in his room." He dug into his pocket then held his palm out, revealing a handful of loose diamonds.

My eyes widened. He had hundreds of thousands of dollars of precious gems in his pocket. As a mom, I couldn't help but wonder what would happen if he had a hole in his pocket. Unfortunately, I didn't have much of a chance to think about it.

"In here," Tyler said, nudging me in the back with the gun. The double barn doors were still open, and he pushed Desi, Goldie, and me into his workshop. He shut the doors behind him, then, with his gun still trained on us, rummaged around in the cabinets with one arm.

When he turned back around to face us, he held lengths of twine. I could hear Desi breathing quickly next to me and Goldie poising himself to pounce on Tyler. If he did, I'm sure Tyler would have shot him, so I patted Goldie's head to relax him.

"What are you going to do to us?" I asked.

"What does it look like, princess? I'm going to tie you up, set this barn on fire, and then hightail it out of town. I'll be halfway to Mexico before they find you in the smoldering rubble."

I flashed back to the condo in Ericksville that had been torched by an arsonist. I'd seen it before the fire crew was able to extinguish all of the flames. The fire had spread terrifyingly fast.

He sat us on the ground next to a support pole and tied

Desi and me back-to-back against the pole. To keep Goldie in place, he tied a length of rope to his collar.

Tyler stepped back, admiring his handiwork. "That should do it." He brushed his hands off and threw the remaining rope in a corner.

I twisted my hands, but the ropes were tight. Unless Desi had something sharp hidden in her clothes, we were out of luck.

He tore open an emergency supply kit and removed two small votive candles. "This should do it. By the time these catch everything on fire, I'll be safely out of the area."

Desi and I watched as he lit them then threw them up into the loft. At the rate they were burning, I estimated it would only be ten minutes max before the flames reached us. With the large quantities of paint and wood stain lined up against the walls, we wouldn't survive long before the whole place went up in flames.

Tyler stared at us. "Did you ladies have purses? I don't want to leave any loose ends."

I nudged Desi's hand with mine. The faster he left the barn, the more time we had to escape.

"I left a beach bag back in the truck," Desi volunteered.

He turned and left, slamming the doors shut with a bang, then sliding the wooden bar into place to lock us in.

As soon as he was out of sight, we struggled against our bonds.

"I can't get this thing loose," Desi said.

The twine cut into my wrists, but I continued to try to work my way out of them. Next to me, Goldie contorted himself trying to gnaw at the makeshift harness.

The wisps of smoke coming from the loft entranced both Desi and me.

"We're not going to be able to get out." Her face had

turned white and her voice held acceptance of our fate. Outside, something crashed against the side of the barn, adding to the fear we felt inside the structure.

"No!" I said. "We've got to figure this out. Let me see if I can work on getting yours loose." I stretched my fingers as far out as they would go, but only succeeded in briefly looping them under the rope around her wrists. She moved an inch closer and I rubbed the twine against a screw that was sticking out of the bottom of the pole.

"What was that?" Desi twisted her head around toward the back of the barn.

"Huh? What do you mean?" The screw cut through a section of the coarse rope.

"I thought I saw someone in the window."

"Adam? Tomàs?" My spirits lifted.

She shook her head. "No. Someone much shorter." She moved her hands and the remaining strands of rope popped loose. "Hey, I'm free." She stretched out along the floor and managed to open a cabinet against the wall. "Bingo," she said, holding up a file saw.

Using the file, Desi made short work of the ropes holding us to the support pole. We ran to the door and banged on it, but the slide bolt held. The only other exits were the window in the back of the barn that only a child could fit through and the window in the loft. Unfortunately, as we'd determined before, there was no way up to the loft from the inside. That didn't really matter, because it was quickly being engulfed by fire. We were stuck.

"Maybe whoever was out there will hear us," Desi said.

"Help us!" we shouted.

"Hold on," a voice came from the other side of the door. "This thing is stuck." The door shook from the exterior, but it didn't open.

Burning embers crashed down from the loft, sending flames that crept closer and closer to where we stood. Goldie barked loudly at the approaching fire. Smoke filled the air and we lowered ourselves to the ground to decrease our exposure.

"Please hurry," I cried out.

With a crack, the bolt slid open and the doors were flung open. Coughing, the three of us spilled out onto the dirt outside, then crawled a few feet away.

"Are you ok?" a woman asked.

I rubbed my eyes to make sure I wasn't seeing something that wasn't there. "Sela?"

She nodded. "I came back to check on you. I think I may have gone too far with taking your dog."

"Ya think?" Desi asked.

I elbowed her. "Well, thank you for rescuing us." My eyes darted around. "Tyler locked us in there and set it on fire. Have you seen him?"

Plumes of smoke were rising from the top of the barn.

"We need to get further away," Desi said.

"Yeah, I saw Tyler." Sela grinned. "Come here."

We skirted the barn, giving it a wide berth. Near Tyler's truck, a body lay on the ground in a crumpled heap.

"What happened?" I asked.

She reached down near the rear right tire and held up a can of spray sunscreen. "I found this in that bag over there when it was still by the old truck." She pointed at Desi's beach bag, lying in the dirt near Tyler. "I heard him threatening you, and when he came back to his truck after grabbing the bag, I jumped out and sprayed him in the face. While he was distracted, I hit him with a tire iron he'd left in a heap in the dirt. Then I tied him up. All that junk he has lying around really came in handy."

"Whoa," Desi said. "That took some guts."

"Yeah." Maybe I'd misjudged Sela. I glanced down at Goldie. Nope, even if she'd saved us, she'd still stolen my dog and put us in this position in the first place.

Sirens pierced the air and the fire truck from the celebration, still decorated in festive blue and yellow ribbons, roared up to the barn. Three firefighters jumped out and quickly trained a hose on the building. A police car followed close behind them.

"And that's my signal to leave." Sela hurried down the path toward the resort.

The police officer got out of his patrol car, quickening his pace when he saw Tyler bound on the ground.

He made his way over to us at the edge of the clearing. "What happened here?"

Desi and I looked at each other.

"It's a long story," she said.

I nodded. "That man over there locked us in the barn and set it on fire."

He looked over to the burning barn and then back to us. His eyes widened. "He tried to kill you?"

"Yes," we said in unison.

He called for backup and went over to Tyler, adding more secure zip ties to his hands. Tyler still hadn't woken up after Sela had hit him on the head with a tire iron.

"So who hit him?" the policeman asked.

"It was a woman named Sela. She works over at the Thunder Lake Resort."

He scanned the clearing. "So where is she now?"

Desi shrugged. "We don't know. She went back there after she got us out of the barn."

I don't think either of us wanted to throw Sela under the

bus for her crimes. She could have been killed saving us from Tyler, but she hadn't run away when she saw we were in danger. I'd talk to Leah afterward and find out if she still wanted to press charges against Sela. Outing her as the camp vandal didn't seem like a decision that should be up to Desi and me.

"Check his pockets," I said. "He had the stolen diamonds in there."

The policeman's eyebrows shot up and he pointed at Tyler. "He's the jewelry store robber?"

"Yes. And he killed Jed. They robbed the store together, but he double-crossed Jed." The adrenaline had worn off and I felt drained.

"He told you that?" he asked.

Desi nodded. "He told us everything before he tried to kill us." She glared at Tyler.

The officer made a few more notes on his pad before his backup arrived. Tyler moved a little, groaning as he stretched. He sat up awkwardly with his hands and feet tied. The policeman went over to him and read him his rights. Another two police cars showed up and two of the officers helped carry Tyler over to the back of a patrol car.

After another officer interviewed us for about twenty minutes, we were given the go-ahead to head back to the resort.

"Do you think anyone noticed we were gone?" I glanced at my watch. About two hours had passed. "You'd think they would have at least noticed I wasn't there to present the medal to the winner of the boat race."

Desi snorted. "I certainly hope so. We were only supposed to be gone for half an hour."

We stopped by our cabins on the way back and found our family gathered on the grassy lawn behind them. The boys were playing with a ball, but the adults were pacing back and forth.

"Jill," Adam called out, running to me. "Where were you?"

Desi hugged Tomàs and he peered at her. "What happened to the two of you?"

I took a deep breath. "Someone stole Goldie and someone else locked us in a barn and set it on fire." I leaned down to pet Goldie and settle my nerves a bit.

"What?" Tomàs yelped.

Adam's eyes bugged out. "Who tried to kill you?"

"Tyler—he lives on the property next door." Desi picked up Lina, who was asleep on a blanket nearby.

"Apparently, he and Jed had robbed the jewelry store and he'd killed Jed to get his share of the diamonds." I leaned against Adam, grateful for his presence.

"And you two just happened to figure that out?" Tomàs narrowed his eyes at Desi.

"No, no. We weren't snooping there this time, I promise." Desi looked straight into her husband's eyes. "We were only there to rescue Goldie, and we got caught up in the mess."

"Well, who dognapped Goldie?" Adam asked.

"Sela." I scanned what I could see of the resort but wasn't surprised not to see her around. If she was smart, she'd be taking Tyler's route toward Mexico at this point.

"The hiking guide?" Tomàs asked.

"Yep." Desi nodded. "She was the one who was creating all the trouble at the resort like setting the boats loose. She wanted Del and Leah to sell so she could have Del to herself." She shook her head. "She was a little wacko, but she did save us from the burning barn."

"I can't believe it." Adam hugged me harder. "It wasn't until you'd been gone for an hour that we really started to get worried. But we didn't want to raise too much of a fuss because of the festivities. We were about to send out a search party when the fire trucks left to respond to the fire next door.

"Are you sure you weren't snooping?" Tomàs asked.

"Nope, Scout's honor." I grinned at him. It wasn't often that I could say Desi and I were completely innocent. Well, at least mostly innocent.

"Why are you so happy?" Adam asked.

"We're alive and together in this beautiful place." I spread my arms out, joy spreading through me as I realized it was true. Desi and I had been in danger, but we were fine now and I didn't want to waste any more of the precious time we had with our families.

Desi laughed. "She's right. Let's get back to the festivities."

Tomàs and Adam gave us dubious looks but gathered up the kids and we went down to the lake where they were now having swimming races.

19

*L*ater that night, Desi and I met with Del and Leah in the deserted café to tell them about what had transpired earlier in the day. Del was there before Leah, and I decided to ask him why Tyler had told me that Del was hiding something.

I looked out the window to make sure Leah wasn't around. "Del, when I talked to Tyler earlier this week, he said something about you having things in your past that Jed wanted to tell people about."

Del smiled. "Oh, that. He's probably talking about my conviction for stealing from a bike shop when I was a teenager. I was under eighteen, so it was expunged from my record." He peered at me. "I never hid it from Leah. In fact, I've been involved with the local youth here and use it as an example of what not to do. If I can keep one kid from ruining their life, I'll be a happy man."

"Oh." I was quiet for a moment. "Thank you for telling me about it. I'm sorry to be so nosy, but I thought if there was something you were hiding from Leah, she should know about it."

"No problem," he said easily. "I understand your concern."

Leah entered the café, and Desi and I gave them the details about what had happened earlier.

"Sela was the one who did all of it? The burned life jackets? The boats that were set loose?" Leah asked, her mouth agape.

"Yeah," Desi said. "She was behind everything."

Leah sat back in her chair. "I can't believe it was her all along. I mean, I thought it could be somebody that worked at the resort, but I wouldn't have guessed it was Sela." She turned to Del. "Would you have thought she would've done that?"

He shook his head. "No. I knew she was a little bit off with the way that she was telling people she was dating me, but that was even crazier than I had expected."

"Well, at least now you don't have to worry about somebody causing more trouble at the resort." I smiled at my friends.

Leah rubbed her thumb over the knuckles on her left hand and looked down at the table. "All of this has just been too much." She cast a quick glance at Del and took a deep breath. "I think it's time to sell the resort."

Del put his hand on her arm and gazed at her with warm brown eyes. "No."

Leah pulled her head back and looked at her soon-to-be ex-husband.

"What do you mean? I thought you wanted to sell the resort."

He smiled. "I did. But everything that's happened has made me re-examine things." He took her hands in his. "Leah, you're my family. If the resort is what you want, let's make it work. All I know is that I love you and I can't see a future for myself without you in it."

Her eyes misted over and she threw her arms around him. "Oh, Del. I don't know if owning the resort is what I see for my future, but I know I want to be with you. We'll figure it out together."

Desi and I looked at each other.

"I think this is our cue to get out of here," she whispered.

A broad smile stretched across my lips. "I think so too."

~

We checked out of the resort exactly at noon and drove home, stopping only once, to buy hamburgers and fries. Still, it was Mikey's bedtime when we arrived home. As soon as we released Goldie from his in-car harness, he ran into the house. Fluffy came running up to see us, claiming she hadn't been fed in a week.

"I know Grandma and Grandpa came over to feed you," I admonished her. "But I'll give you a treat." I snuggled her close, which she tolerated in order to get her treat.

Adam carried Ella in and Mikey milled around, still groggy from falling asleep in the car.

"Time for bed for you, mister." I offered my hand to him and led him upstairs to brush his teeth and put on pajamas.

"Ok." He didn't put up much of a fight and fell asleep immediately after crawling into bed.

Once both kids were down, Adam and I looked at each other.

"I hate to say it, but if you don't mind, I'd like to check on work," he said sheepishly.

I laughed. "I was about to say the same thing."

He retired to his study and I called Beth, who was home from the office.

"Hey, how did everything go with the event yesterday?" she asked. "We fed the pets this morning and everything seemed fine at your house." She sounded better than she had earlier in the week, although her voice was hoarse.

"It is. Thank you for watching over everything. Are you feeling better?" I sat back in my desk chair. She'd probably find out what had happened to Desi and me on our vacation, but I wasn't going to tell her about it. Beth had enough to worry about without knowing her daughter and daughter-in-law had almost been killed.

"I feel much better. I told you not to worry—it was just a little summer cold." She cleared her throat. "Although, I am glad that you're back to deal with Angela. I'm really starting to regret offering up the Boathouse for the haunted house."

"I know. But keep reminding yourself of all the good publicity. Goodness knows we could use it after the murder investigation there over the summer." I got up and went into the kitchen to pour myself a healthy portion of Chardonnay.

"You're probably right, but I can still gripe about it, right?" Beth laughed. "Anyway, everything else is fine. I'll see you tomorrow, ok?"

"Sounds good. Thanks again for taking care of things here."

We said our goodbyes and I hung up the phone, taking my wine out to the deck to gaze out at the setting sun. As the sun sank down on the horizon, flooding the sky with pinks, purples, and glowing orange, I contemplated the end of summer. The last few months had been an exciting time for our family. Adam had quit his job and started his own practice and I'd gone to work at the Boathouse.

I'd managed some challenging events there, and I was

sure there would be many more in my future, but I was happy to have made the jump back into the workforce— even if it meant dealing with people like Angela Laveaux. I could feel my blood pressure rising just thinking about her, so I sipped my wine and forced myself to relax. After all, how bad could one demanding woman and her haunted house be?

How bad could Angela and her haunted house be? Find out in MURDEROUS MUMMY WARS, coming in October 2018.

Thank you for reading Stuck With S'More Death. I hope

you enjoyed spending more time with Jill Andrews and her family. If you did, I'd really appreciate it if you left a review.

For information about my new releases and other exciting news, please visit my website, nicoleellisauthor.com and sign up for my e-mail newsletter.

BOOKS BY NICOLE ELLIS

Jill Andrews Cozy Mysteries
 Brownie Points for Murder - Book #1
 Death to the Highest Bidder - Book #2
 A Deadly Pair O'Docks - Book #3
 Stuck with S'More Death - Book #4
 Murderous Mummy Wars - Book #5 Coming October 2018

Candle Beach Sweet Romances
 Sweet Beginnings - Book #1
 Sweet Success - Book #2
 Sweet Promises - Book #3
 Sweet Memories - Book #4
 Sweet History - Book #5 Coming September 2018

Fortune's Bay
 A Map to Destiny

Made in the USA
Las Vegas, NV
07 August 2021